Figure

By
Ken Kirkberry

CONTENTS

Ken Kirkberry is a lifelong daydreamer who has finally placed his thoughts into print.

Ken has been brought up on Sci-Fi in both print and film format. Ken is devoted to his family and friends.

Through the Enlightenment trilogy of books these views are explored. However, with a second love of crime and fantasy Ken has, with this book taken on a new genre – Crime.

Chapter One

The Execution

Raspin Fernandez was coming round; his head hurt. Opening his eyes he took a deep breath, all was black. Raspin tried to move his arms but they would not move, *what was happening?* He thought. Eyes fully open, head cleared, Raspin could tell he was in a mask of some sort. Although not clear he could just tell there was some light through whatever was covering his head. The light moved—someone was moving around him.

"Who's there?" There was no reply. Raspin tried his hands again, they would not move. Raspin felt someone grab him, pulling his trunk upwards. He was now kneeling. "Who's there?" Raspin shouted again. Raspin could sense a person moving around him. "Tell me who the fuck is there?" Raspin moved his head from side to side trying to keep up with the moving figure.

"I'm the last voice you will hear."

Raspin thought, *I know that voice*. Raspin continued to think, but stopped as he felt the end of a gun at his temple. His last thoughts went as the bang cleared his head.

The shower water was warm and steamy; Detective John Mercer was getting ready for another day's work in the New York Police Department. Mercer walked out of the shower to the basin and looked in the large mirror in front of him. Looking back at him was a dark haired thirty year old, well built he thought. Looking closer, the last few years had added a few pounds and the knife and bullet wound in his chest were reminders of how hard being a New York cop was. Deep in thought his ringing cell disturbed him. "Mercer. How you doing, Ray?"

"Hi John, don't go to the station, come straight to the docks, the Old Red Hook's fish building. There's been a homicide; meet you there."

Mercer needed no more information; he dressed and was soon out in the New York traffic heading for the docks. Siren and lights blaring and he arrived at the scene quite quickly. "Hi Mercer, your partner got here first, he is inside."

"Thanks Dobbs."

Mercer entered the old building, his first sight being a car with both front doors open and his colleagues busying around the front of it. Mercer moved to the front, noting the smashed cell phone on the floor. Standing over the body was his partner Detective Sergeant Ray Freemond. Ray was an Afro-American in his fifties and had been Mercer's partner for over five years. "Hi Ray, do we know who it is?"

"Guess only, the car is Raspin Fernandez's. The hood on his head, or what's left of it, does not help."

Mercer moved closer to the body, taking in the head, then the tied arms. "That tattoo on his left hand, its Fernandez alright."

Freemond looked over, "I'm glad one of us is awake. You are right but let the forensic bods confirm it." Freemond nodded to the door. Mercer looked at the door, four suited up C.S.I. team members were approaching.

"Morning Lisa, how are you?"

"Hi Ray, John. I'm good. What do you have for us?"

Mercer looked at Lisa Barrett, a pretty looking brunette in her late twenties. Lisa was a close friend as well as a colleague. "We believe it is Raspin Fernandez. Our guess, a gang execution by the way he is tied and the shot through the head."

Barrett smirked, "Wow John, now I know why you are the detective. Get away from the body and let us do our bit to confirm that."

Mercer and Freemond moved away and walked to Officer Dobbs. "Who found him?"

"The dock worker in the office over there, saw the door ajar on this derelict site so walked in and got the shock of his life, Ray."

"Thanks," Freemond looked at Mercer. "I'll talk to him, you look around."

Mercer walked around the scene. There appeared to be little sign of a struggle, inside there were no C.C.T.V. cameras. Moving outside Mercer looked around further then sat against the trunk of his car to wait for his partner.

"He doesn't know anything, poor guy. Very upset as not often you find a dead body." Freemond informed as he leaned on the car next to Mercer.

"A few C.C.T.V. cameras but none are where we want to see. I've asked the tech team to bring up what they can. Most appear to be general cameras or traffic ones at the entrance and up the road. You had breakfast?"

"Of course Gloria, always…oh, sorry buddy."

4

"Don't be, let's get a coffee at least."

Coffee break over the two detectives was at their station just after noon. Mercer went to the tech team first. Although being quite a short period they had picked up images of the car, none showed any internal or external images of use. "We can't follow the full journey of the car but I'm sure we could if we called the Carnellos." Mercer said as he sat at his desk opposite his partner, who was also sitting. "Fernandez was one of theirs but they won't help us."

"And you won't be bothered to ask?" Captain Mark Ward spoke. A near sixty year old, average size but stocky, his beer belly was his most obvious physical feature.

Freemond looked up, "Hi Captain, I didn't see you there."

"Obviously, my office ten minutes. Call Lisa and get her up here as well. I want an update."

Mercer and Freemond said no more but made the call and collected what they had ready for the meeting. Barrett was on time and all three entered the captain's office.

"One Desert Eagle .50 calibre through the head. Looks as though the perp was in the back of the car, pistol whipped Fernandez first then drove him to the docks to execute him. Around two this morning."

"Wow Lisa, that's good in a few hours. His head must have been in pieces, how can you tell he was pistol whipped?" Mercer asked.

"The blood marks in the car. You're right I can't get much off the head. Dental records and fingerprints confirm it was Fernandez though. No obvious perp fingerprints, gloves were worn and the cell, although smashed, is a burn phone."

Mercer spoke, "So, we won't get access to any of the messages as they will be encrypted. Any calls will probably be to other burn phones and the like?"

"Yes, standard nowadays. The government need to change the rules around encrypted messages or access for us forensics, especially in murder investigations. Unlikely the perp called or communicated with the vic anyway, but we will look at it."

"And you two. What have you got?"

"Nothing on the C.C.T.V. yet captain," Mercer replied.

"So that's it, three of my best officers and we have nothing. What about witnesses or family?"

"Captain, no apparent witnesses and that scumbag had no family," Freemond was quite forthright.

"Look, he may have been a scumbag but you are homicide cops, get out and do something!"

"You heard from Carnello yet, Captain?" Mercer asked.

"No, strange but we all know Carnello will not show his hand in any way unless he has to. Besides it clearly was an execution so Carnello is probably behind it. Are you all still here?"

Barrett, Freemond and Mercer got the message and left the office. Back at their desks, Barrett started, "Guys, I know Carnello is the biggest gangster in town but we do need to be serious."

"I am being serious but there is nothing to go on," Freemond said defensively.

"Lisa, you said it looks professional, no forensics of any use will be found so it is a bit of a loose end."

"I expect better of you, John, but yes I doubt we will find much. How about a drink on the way home?"

"Yeah that would be good, I'll catch you in your office in about half hour. Ray, you coming?"

"Not tonight sorry. We are babysitting our granddaughter."

Half hour later Mercer was in the forensics' office and Barrett was at her P.C. "I thought we were getting a beer?"

"Yeah sure, just need the ladies room," Barrett rose to go to the toilet.

"Can I use your P.C.? Need to check something."

"Yes but if you get a bug or something I will be angry."

Mercer smiled and went about the keyboard. Barrett returned, "What are you looking smug about? I will hurt you if you have done something to my P.C."

"Look at the printer."

Barrett went to the printer and pulled out the printed page. Smiling she turned to Mercer. "The new plush restaurant on Fifth Avenue are giving discounts already?"

"Yep. That voucher will allow us a meal there even on our salary."

"Got to be within this month, when are you thinking of going?"

"Let's decide over that drink."

It was a short walk to the Irish bar that most of the station frequented. Barrett and Mercer were well known to the barman and owner Sean Murphy. A couple of Guinness's passed and Barrett thought this was the right time. "So, are you ready to go out? That voucher is to be used within the month."

Mercer thought, "Yes, I think I am, after all, it is just a meal."

"That is good, how are you doing?"

Mercer looked at his friend, she was probably one of a few that could ask him outright. "Nearly two years now and it still hurts," Mercer had a tear in his eye.

"You need to talk about it, that is what the psychiatrist advised."

"I know but…even with friends like you, Lisa, it is hard. Look, I need to go."

"I'm sorry, John, please?"

"No, no problem. I need to go." With that Mercer rose, gave Barrett a quick kiss on the cheek and left.

Murphy approached Barrett, standing behind the bar asked, "Is he still having trouble talking about it?"

"Yes. Losing your wife and baby has got to be hard, Murph."

"Lisa, don't be upset, you, more than anyone, is helping him get over it."

"I know, but will he ever do you think?"

"He has to some how, just to live. Look, I'll give him a call and take him to a game one evening, that meal he was talking about with you is a big step."

"Yes. Give me something stronger. One for the road as they say."

Chapter Two

Grief

Mercer was in early the next day having already checked with the tech team that there was no further evidence. Freemond arrived late, and on entering the squad room asked " Traffic is getting worse and I had to drop Toni off at school, her car had broken down."

"Hey, I'm not checking, buddy, how is your daughter?"

"She is good, hates leaving the little one each morning but that's what grandma's are for. Gloria loves having Charlotte. How did it go with Lisa last night?"

"Yeah fine, just a couple of beers and I went home."

"If you go out tonight I'll have a Friday drink with you both."

"No, not tonight."

Freemond looked at his partner, "You having a problem, buddy? Do you want to talk?"

"No. Look, I need the bathroom," Mercer rose and left.

Barrett entered the squad room, Freemond addressed her, "Morning Lisa, you just missed him. Bad night last night?"

"Morning Ray. No it was ok but John was a little on edge. I asked about, well, went to talk about Tanya and Maddie but he just closed up and left."

"Losing your whole family in a car crash is hard, what two years now?"

"Wait, that's what he said. When was it? I mean what date…no wait, let me think." Barrett thought deep, "Oh no, we are fools!"

"Why, what are you on about?"

"Tomorrow would be Maddie's third birthday."

Ray dropped his head, and then looked up to see his partner coming back to the desk. "Hey buddy, I…I don't know what to say."

Barrett did not say anything but grasped Mercer giving him a little hug. "You worked it out. Tomorrow would have been my little girls third birthday."

"Do you have anything planned?" Barrett let Mercer go as she spoke.

"I intend to go to the grave then drive round some places we used to go."

"If you want company I will go with you?"

Mercer looked at Lisa, "No, thank you. I want to do it on my own."

"What about Tanya's parents?" Freemond asked carefully.

"Tanya's parents are in Florida now, you know that. I will call them though."

Lisa sat on the desk next to the seated Mercer. "And your mom?"

Mercer looked up, gave a sigh and replied. "Mom is doing well in the home, yes, maybe I should see her. Do you guys want coffee?" Barrett and Freemond both nodded yes. Mercer left the room.

"This is hard Ray, I really want to help him but…"

"Lisa, his father died of cancer about five years ago and it turned his mother mad with grief. Then that awful tragedy, his wife and child killed in a car crash. I love him but I also struggle." Freemond gave Barrett's hand a little grasp. Barrett gave Freemond a smile and sat in the vacant chair. Mercer returned, three cups of coffee to hand and no one spoke as he distributed them out and sat next to Barrett on his own desk.

Captain Ward approached, looking quite agitated. "What am I paying you three for—another coffee break?"

As the captain went to speak again, Barrett made some shush motions to her lips with one hand, pointing at the paper calendar on the desk, all behind Mercer's back. The captain stopped, thought and fell in. "I mean coffee is good for the brain, how about an update in twenty." With this he went to his office.

Twenty minutes passed and they all entered the office. Barrett went first. "As we thought Fernandez was struck in the car, driven to the building and tied up. Once he came round the perp shot him, execution style. There was no struggle and little, if any, evidence left for us to work with."

Freemond looked at Mercer who was looking out the window. "To be honest, Captain, we have nothing much either. My thoughts, an inside punishment from Carnello."

"You don't like Carnello much do you Ray," The captain stated.

"My Toni teaches at the school where many of his employees as such come from. Fernandez may be of no real loss but he and many before leave behind family. Toni has had to deal with many young siblings of murdered gang members."

"We still have to do our job," Mercer addressed all present.

"I know John. Look, there is no point talking to Fernandez's family, if he has any, or friends but maybe Demis might have something."

Mercer thought—Demis was a Greek-Italian bar owner that had many a link to the gang world; he was their best informant. "Worth a shot—let's go."

"Freemond, Barrett go. Mercer, wait a minute."

His two colleagues left the room as Mercer looked at the captain. "Look John, I know what day it is, well, tomorrow at least. Should you be here?"

"Yes Captain, I'm ok, working helps."

"Are you sure? You're not only one of my best but I count you as a friend too."

"Thanks Captain. It's only today and then it's my weekend off so I will be ok." With that Mercer left the office.

Catching his partner up, they headed to Demis's bar. Nothing was said on the short journey until they pulled up at outside the bar. "Amazing, a coffee bar during the day frequented by normal people like us, then at night a drinks bar for the bad of New York." Mercer laughed at his partner's comment, leading them in towards a booth near the window where both men sat. Demis was tall, older than Freemond and Greek looking with his dark hair and tanned complexion. His mother was Greek and his father was Italian, he had been brought up in Greece until his father's work moved from Scilly to New York.

"How are my two favourite detectives?" Demis asked whilst handing out a couple of coffees.

"We are good, how's business?"

"Good Mercer, good. Nearly as busy as you guys."

Freemond chuckled, "You know why we are here, certainly not for the coffee if that's what you call it."

"Cheek man, and you have never paid!" Demis looked indignant.

"I'll drink it but you talk while I drink."

Demis sat next to Mercer and in a low voice said, "Look, all is strange, no one seems to know anything. There are a lot of people asking questions but no one is answering."

"Is it an internal dispute?"

"No Ray, I don't think so. To the outside world the shutters are up but to us…I mean, well, you know. If Carnello did it for a reason we would know, keeps up the fear."

"What about Frith, it's his type of thing?"

Demis looked at Mercer, then thought. "Years ago maybe but even Frith would not do such a thing directly."

"But he could have one of his minions do it?"

"Of course, but again there would be noise and I am not hearing it. Maybe it is just too soon."

"So, info zilch, payment zilch!" Freemond laughed and got up. "Let us know when you do hear anything."

"I will," Demis shook Mercer's hand as he rose. "Of course I may not be around any longer if all of my customers fail to pay." Mercer and Freemond laughed, knowing Demis would be laughing behind them.

Returning to the station did not help; both detectives were struggling to think of a next step. The hours went by slowly but eventually home time was upon them. Barrett entered the office and again sat on Mercer's desk next to him.

"You sure you don't want company tomorrow?"

"No thanks. I need to handle it in my own way."

"Look, if Saturday is out then maybe you both can come over to ours for Sunday lunch?"

"I like that Ray, I'm in. John?"

"Maybe."

"Come on buddy, tomorrow will be tough, spend some time with your friends away from this place. 1pm we will be expecting you both." With that Freemond left.

"We are all just looking out for you, John, it will be fun."

"I know." Mercer rose gave Barrett a peck on the cheek, "I'll try to make it."

Mercer pulled the car up at the side of the cemetery, the weather had turned cold and rain was in the air. Neither mattered as he walked the short walk to the graveside. Two graves, two grave stones, one bigger than the other. Mercer knelt between the two and pulled out the old flowers on his wife's grave, replacing with new, red roses. Turning to his daughter's grave he removed the single red rose and again replaced it. Tears came to his eyes as he unwrapped the box he had brought; taking the pink teddy bear out Mercer hugged it then placed it against the gravestone. Kneeling for some time, oblivious to the now stronger rain around him, Mercer looked at the names and the dates and said aloud, "Happy birthday my sweet baby."

"You poor man you are soaked," Nurse Wright said as Mercer entered the reception area of the nursing home.

"I'm ok, I've come to see Mom," Mercer replied.

"I know Mr Mercer, no it is Detective Mercer?" Nurse Wright said with a smile.

"You know I'm a cop, I've been here many times."

Nurse Wright giggled, "Your mom is fine, in her usual chair out back near the window. You go in and I'll get you both a hot drink."

"Thanks." Mercer entered the main room and headed for the window. Standing a few feet from his mom he looked at her. Although only in her early sixties Steph Mercer looked much older, the early death of her beloved husband had taken its toll.

"Hi Mom."

"Hi Johnny, sit with me."

Mercer did as requested. "How has your week been, Mom?"

"Oh fine, I won at the bingo you know."

"That's great. Oh thank you," Nurse Wright had provided the drinks.

"She is one of the nice ones…the others…" Steph hesitated. "The others are witches!"

"Mom, I'm sure they are not."

"You don't have to live with them! Anyway, why are you on your own, where is Tanya? I have not seen her for some time."

Mercer held back his tears, "Mom, Tanya has gone, and you know that."

Steph thought, "Gone where, surely she has time to see me?"

Mercer continued the conversation but each question and answer got more difficult. Finally saying goodbye and promising to visit soon Mercer went to leave. Before leaving he grabbed Nurse Wright.

"Mom is no better?"

"She is fine in herself, indeed quite healthy in physical terms. But no, she is no better mentally. A shock like that then…you know it seems too much for her. How are you doing?"

Mercer thought, "I have good and bad days, today being a bad one."

"If you need help we have people here."

"No, thank you. I've had my fair share of shrinks but thank you."

Chapter Three

Another Murder

"Turn the music up, man. I love working late Saturdays!" Gonzalez shouted at his driver. Timo obliged, the music blared out. Gonzalez boogied in his seat, singing to the music. Timo drove a half-mile and pulled into the kerb, turning the music down. "Hey man, I was enjoying that!"

"Do your job."

Gonzalez sat up straight and wound down the window, two men on the sidewalk walked towards the car. "Hey brother, give me the money!"

"Look, Gonz, we don't have enough to live on, please?"

"No way bro, you took the stuff, you pay the money."

"Give us another week, or maybe we pay half now?"

Timo moved in his seat, his side arm clearly visible. Gonzalez looked at his partner then looked back at the two in his window. "Come on bro, you don't want to make my man unhappy." Gonzalez removed his own gun from his belt. "Me neither!" The two men looked at each other, pulled some notes from their trousers and handed the money over to Gonzalez. "If it's not all there we will come back for a finger then toes for every dollar missing."

Timo laughed and drove the car off the kerb onto the pavement, there was no traffic on the dark rain washed street. A quarter of mile and he stopped at a red light. Gonzalez hit the music button.

"Shit man, what was that?" Gonzalez turned to look out the back window.

"Some fuck has gone into the back of us!" Timo screamed as he exited the car. Walking along side his car he saw the hooded figure standing behind the open door of the car behind. Reaching the trunk of his car, he saw the car behind embedded in it. "Shit man, you bumped me. Do you know who I am?"

The figure did not speak, raising a gun from behind the door, he took aim and…bang! Timo hit the pavement. Gonzalez was on the other side of the car adjacent to the trunk and going for his gun. Another bang and Gonzalez fell. The figure moved around the door, looked down at Timo's body, slid over the trunk and looked down at Gonzalez's body. Breaking into a sprint the figure disappeared into an alley between two clubs.

"Ray, are you listening to me?" Mercer shouted down his mobile.

"Yes, John, I am but you need to calm down."

"Calm down, I've just got up and the local news is talking about a gang land slaying in the Bronx. You are there, why didn't you call me?"

"I'm not there now, I'm at the station. Yes, there was a shooting around 2am this morning. Despatch called me and I told them to leave you, John, you were at your child's grave yesterday, come on."

Mercer paused, "That's not the point, I was in and asleep early, I could have come over. I am your partner remember. I'm coming over!"

Freemond did not bother with responding with, *it's a Sunday, you are off and really need some time to yourself.* Barrett walked up to Freemond. "Was that John? There is no reason for him to have been there."

"I know, but he is on his way here now."

"No. Don't tell him I've been out all night as well, he will freak!"

"I would get your forensics in gear and maybe talk to him with at least something. Let me write my report."

Mercer ignored the desk sergeant's greetings and went straight to his partner's desk. "What's happened, the radio suggests a couple dead at least?"

"Morning Ray, how are you?" Ray joked.

Mercer kicked his chair, retrieved it then sat down. "We are partners, you should have called regardless!"

"I am not going to answer that, you needed a lay in if not more time off."

"It's 10am, that's a lay in on a Sunday, what happened?"

"Ok. Looks like Timo and Gonzalez were popped last night, around 2am. Single big shot to the head is my guess."

"Executed like Fernandez-our perp?"

"No, no. The guy drove into the back of them and shot them both as they exited the car at the lights near the Birdcage club."

"So not our perp?"

"My guess is yes, a Desert Eagle for sure, just got to finish and confirm they are the same shells!" Barrett called as she walked towards her colleagues.

"You got the call too, no one bothered to call me. A team? Not!"

"You deserved your sleep. Ray and I have handled it but are knackered so maybe you could write it up," Barrett ended with her best smile.

Freemond stood and threw his notes at Mercer, "Now that's a good idea. There was a witness, a drunken bum so no real use. The tech guys are looking at C.C.T.V. so maybe there will be something there." Heading towards the door he added, "Oh, the perp's car is registered to Meekson, that two bit druggie on the Bronx. Uniform are there and forensics but I doubt he would have anything to do with it. See you at one!"

Barrett looked at Mercer, his mouth dropped and his eyes wide staring at the swinging door that Freemond had just left through. "John, how was yesterday?"

Mercer looked up at the still smiling Barrett. "It was good, I saw the graves and mom."

"How was she?"

"She is fine!"

"Be like that!" Barrett turned to walk out, shouting back, "1pm dinner, remember!"

Mercer ignored the call and got straight into his partner's notes. Some ten minutes later he rose, grabbed his coat and headed for the tech room. "Anything yet, guys?"

"Hi Merce. Yes but not much use, look."

Mercer looked at the screen, there was a frozen picture of a hooded man running into an alley, the Birdcage in shot behind him. "Can you blow it up?"

"We have tried, he is tracked virtually from the car but the quality is crap. There is little light and lots of rain. I fear we have no chance."

"Keep looking, if he went into the alley he must have come out. Let me know, ok."

"Yep, you will be the first."

Mercer drove to the Bronx and Meekson's house, he had been there before. Meekson was indeed a known drug user come little league supplier. Acknowledging the two uniformed cops outside, Mercer entered the small rundown property. Meekson jumped to his feet as he saw Mercer. "Thank god, a cop I can trust. Arrest me. Look, I have drugs aplenty. I'll show you!" Meekson was pulling at a drawer in the sideboard.

"Thank god you're here, Mercer, he has wanted to be arrested since I've been here!"

"Hi Tate, any forensics? Meekson, shut up or I'll shoot you let alone arrest you!"

Tate laughed, "No, been through the whole place. He was drugged up when the uniforms got here around 3am. I was here about 5 and he is in no shape to have done anything. But the video captured on his crap C.C.T.V. shows a hooded figure coming out of his door and driving off around midnight."

"So our perp came from here. Will Meekson know him?"

"No, my guess is he was out of it and the perp came in through the bathroom window, no lock and does not shut. Took the keys and left through the front."

"A good picture I hope?"

"No, as I said a crap C.C.T.V. but I'll get it to the station and see what we can do. Good luck with him," with that Tate left.

"You are going to arrest me?"

"Why do you want to be arrested?"

"You kidding, two Carnello hoodlums dead and my car involved. I don't have a chance man!"

"Look, they are not stupid, they know you wouldn't kill anyone."

"You kidding man, what if they think I'm involved? Hell, shit, I've got a bat here somewhere, you are gonna have to arrest me when I split your head!"

"Leave it, come on. You are under arrest." Mercer led Meekson out of the door. Mercer addressed the uniforms, "Put him in the can for the rest of the day and tonight. Threatening a police officer will do for now." Mercer handed over the suspect to the uniforms then drove back to the station.

Mercer ignored his cell ringing on the desk beside him. Mercer was more interested in his screen, one of the tech team were leaning over his desk showing him the video. "The camera gets the bottom of the cars...there! Gonzalez hits the pavement. Our perp and Timo were on the other side out of sight. But look, his legs then his body running virtually to the camera then into the alley."

"Come on, that could be anyone. It's dark, poorly lit and it's raining!"

"What you want, Miracles, Merce?"

"No, just a glimpse of the scumbag's face would be nice."

"What have you missed about being a detective? If it was that easy we wouldn't need you," The tech guy laughed. "Seriously, that's all we have, he seemed to go in but not come out any of the other streets leading from the alley."

"So he changed, or maybe lives there?"

"Doubt it, most properties above are store rooms for the crap bars in the area."

"Have we checked them?"

"Uniform have been there all day, ask them."

"Thanks, let me look through this lot first."

Mercer studied the video a few more times and read and reread his partner's notes.

"Hey Merce will you answer your damn cell, Ray's after you, something about dinner?"

"Yeah, yeah. I'm on my way."

Mercer took the car but instead of heading left for his partner's house he headed right towards the Birdcage, pulling up at the sidewalk just outside the club. "Afternoon guys, anything?"

"Hi Merce. No, we've been up and down this bloody alley numerous times. Some of our team are still up in the buildings above. It's Sunday, cold and raining, we should be home with our families."

Mercer gave the cop a smile then addressed the uniform standing next to him, "A witness, you know anything about a witness?"

"Him, can't you hear him? Over there." Mercer looked in the direction the cop was pointing. A tramp was clearly calling and waving to them. "Four coffees so far and he has zilch!"

Mercer laughed, "Are they fresh coffees you both have?"

"Yeah, well, five minutes ago we just got them before you arrived."

"Good, thank you, looks like the tramp's fifth's on its way," Mercer took both cups before heading to the tramp, ignoring the protests from behind.

"Thank you. Thank you."

"I hear this is your fifth."

"Who's counting? Warming my hands is more important than drinking it."

Mercer knelt next to the sitting tramp. "So what's your story?"

"Military, injured in the middle east. No home, left to rot."

Mercer thought for a second, "Look buddy, I'm sorry, we should treat our heroes better. Maybe you could tell me what happened and I might have a contact that can help you?"

"As I told lots of you earlier. I heard a crash, looked up, some hooded guy from the rear car took out the two from the front, right there at the lights."

"You said the hooded guy was military to my partner earlier?"

"The way he held the gun, one shot each, blew their heads off. You never forget the sound of a Desert Eagle or miss its power."

Mercer looked at the tramp; maybe he was a military hero. "Sorry to ask again but did you see his face?"

"Looked like a black. I don't know. I wish I had, worth at least a meal from you guys. Hey wait, yes, I did, can I see one of your drawing guys at the station maybe?"

Mercer laughed, "Sorry buddy, you missed that one. Look, here is a twenty and a card for a friend of mine.

She runs a mission two blocks up that way, do you know it?"

"Thanks for the money, but no, I fell out with the mission for arguing. I won't be let in."

"Look, I'll give Mary a call and let her know you are coming. She will let you in. What's your name?"

"Private Reynolds."

Mercer stood, stopped, pulled another 20 dollars out and dropped it to Reynolds's hand before walking off. "All the boys finished now?"

"Yeah, nothing, we are calling it a day. You owe us two coffees."

Mercer laughed and got in his car, as he went to pull away he shouted through the open side window at his uniformed colleagues. "Daylight robbery I'd say, call the cops!"

Morning came, as the captain entered his office, "Wake up Mercer before I throw your arse out of my office!"

Mercer opened his eyes; Captain Ward was in his face. "Sorry Captain. Your office couch was too comfortable, I must have slept here all night," Mercer was very apologetic.

"Get out of here, you've made my office stink!"

Mercer moved quick, grabbed a coffee and sat at his desk.

"So you were working all night, that's your excuse?"

"Morning Ray, my excuse for what?"

"Missing dinner at my place yesterday!"

"I'm sorry buddy, honest, but I was working. All day in fact, fell asleep in the captain's office."

Freemond looked at Mercer, the captain's office then back to Mercer. "Really that's funny maybe I'll let you off this time. Lisa enjoyed it."

"Lisa turned up?"

"Yes, albeit closer to four than one but we had a good time. She likes you, you should give her a chance."

"She is nice, but look it's only been two years."

"I'm not saying marry her fool but at least take her out, spend some time with her."

"I will, you want to see and hear what has been found?"

Freemond sat next to his partner; Mercer went through the videos and his findings of the day before. An email from forensics had confirmed the same gun had been used on Fernandez. It was the same perp.

"All interesting stuff but it does not get us any further, buddy," Freemond stood.

"Maybe you are not looking close enough!"

"Hi Lisa, good morning, or is it afternoon yet?"

"Ha ha, it's only ten, Ray."

"What have you got sweetheart?" Mercer gave his best smile.

"You look like shit!"

"Thanks!"

"He slept here all night in the captain's office," Freemond laughed.

Barrett giggled, "Impressive, when is the leaving party?"

"A group leaving party if you don't tell us what you have found Barrett!" The captain had joined the group.

"Yes Captain, of course," Barrett drew a breath. "Not much but we have studied the video further. Look at his movement, speed and overall shape. Guess, male, twenty to thirty, fairly well built, around 6 foot."

"And that helps how?"

Barrett's smile dropped, "It's a start."

"Why male?" Ray thought he would help.

"Look at the build, no boobs from what I can see," Mercer chuckled.

Barrett gave him a dirty look, "Sorry Captain, but yes that's it. No better pictures, no evidence, D.N.A., nothing. The guy is good."

"Congratulating our perpetrator is not what I pay you for, naming them would be useful!" Barrett took a few steps away from the smouldering captain.

"Be easy Captain, they can only work with what they have. No different to us and we have zilch."

"Freemond that sucks. You are one of my best detectives and you have nothing. I'm sure if it weren't a bunch of two bit hoodlums being shot you would have more drive to solve this quicker?"

Freemond rose to his feet, towering above the much shorter captain. Before he could open his mouth Barrett jutted in. "Come on guys, we are all on the same side, long hours and all that." Freemond chose not to speak but headed out of the room, the captain went to his office. "Wow, I really thought Ray was going to lose it." Barrett added.

"Yeah, he did look like it. Do you think the captain has a point?" Mercer said.

"What? Is Ray fumbling it?"

"I don't know but he hates Carnello and his thugs. You know his daughter teaches at one of the hood's schools."

"Yeah I know, but, no, Ray is a good cop. Besides, you are his partner, so are you slacking?"

"No, you know me. Detective of the year, loads of commendations." Mercer said sarcastically.

"Is that an advert for a date?"

Mercer took a gulp but looked at Barrett closely. She was a good-looking, shapely woman. Mercer went to speak, but Barrett continued, "The voucher you fool, the meal?"

"Oh yeah. Yes, of course, whenever, I look forward to it. I better find my partner." Mercer gave Barrett a peck on the cheek and left.

Mercer found his partner sitting on a bench on the small green opposite the station. "You nearly lost it buddy, with the captain?"

"I know. That would have been silly. I like him, hell, I call him a friend." Freemond replied.

"He is under pressure, you know that."

"I know, but accusing me of not doing my job?"

"Hey, that could be thrown at me as well, we are partners."

"How long since the two on Sunday, what thirty hours or so and no show from Carnello or his troops? Something is not right."

Mercer sat next to his partner. "What are you thinking?"

"Gut feel. With that tramp's comment, the guys a pro. Definitely military. No real noise, I mean, no one knee capped, no other gang shootings or violence. Carnello is cleaning up his gang."

"Shouldn't we be talking to the victim's family and friends?"

"Why? Three murders, the connection being Carnello. Come on, even if they had worthwhile family or friends they would be scared of Carnello, they won't talk."

"Look, it's standard procedure. Timo has a brother and parents near my old neighbourhood, it's worth a try."

Mercer and Freemond got in the car and drove to Timo's parent's house, meeting his brother at the door. Mercer being the first to speak. "Dez, I'm sorry about your brother."

"No you're not. You're a cop, you don't care about us!"

"Murder is murder and there is always a victim, of course we care." Freemond had to look away as his partner said this. Before Dez could reply the front door opened and his father walked out.

"Son, your mother needs help with the grandkids. I will deal with these two badges." Dez went inside. "You can't help us!"

"Mr Tamazin, your eldest son was murdered, finding the killer is how we can help you. Surely you want that?"

"Detective Mercer, yes?" Mercer nodded. "Maybe you are too young, things do not work that way. Freemond you know better."

Freemond answered, "Only if we let things stay as they are, someone has to help us change things?"

Mr Tamazin thought, "My wife is in there with Timo's two young kids and a broken hearted mother. One death in the family is hard enough to take."

"Mr Tamazin, it needs people like you to stand up to the likes of Carnello otherwise it will never change."

Mr Tamazin studied Mercer, "You come from the other side of the railway track. It may literally be only a mile from here but it's millions of miles away in culture. I need to protect the rest of my family."

"We can offer protection or even anonymity."

"Son, you have a lot to learn. Freemond, enlighten your partner. I have a funeral to arrange." Mr Tamazin turned, walked through the door and closed it.

Mercer and Freemond walked back to the car and got in. "Damn!" Mercer hit the steering wheel as he spoke. "They know something, their son has been murdered and they won't help. Unbelievable."

"John, you are not wet behind the ears."

"I know, but...let's go home."

Chapter Four

Unlikely Assistance

Mercer was at his desk early, Freemond provided the coffees as his penance for being late again. Neither spoke but studied the evidence on their desks.

"Morning both!"

"Hi Lisa, you are going to tell us you have cleaned the pictures up and we can get the bad guy?"

"You trying to be as lazy as Ray now?" Mercer chuckled; Freemond gave Barrett a dirty look. "No, sorry, still zilch. Cell records don't give much either." Barrett caught the captain opening his office door in the corner of her eye, "Watch out!"

"Mercer, Freemond, my office!" Mercer and Freemond obliged and entered the captain's office, Barrett in tow. Barrett sat against the window to watch. "Did I say Barrett?"

"No Captain but I am a part of the case."

"What if this had nothing to do with the case, it could have been personnel?"

"Moral support then."

The captain rolled his eyes, "Ok, stay. You two, anything new?"

"No Captain," both responded in unison.

"Then maybe I can assist. Carnello wants to see you in his office."

"Us, wow, when?"

"Two hours ago, Merce you're an idiot. Get moving, be careful and don't wind him up. The son of a bitch has a quicker line to the mayor than I do!"

Mercer and Freemond made the trip to Carnello's plush offices on Madison Avenue taking the lift to the twentieth floor. As they exited two heavies stopped them.

"Give me your guns!"

"How about I give you this," Mercer flashed his badge.

The heavy looked at it, ignored the badge and demanded, "Guns!"

"No chance, stop me!" Freemond pushed past and went to the door and entered the office, Mercer followed. Carnello was sat at his desk, his short fat frame filling the chair, cigar smoke swirling around him. Mercer counted four other heavies around the room, heavy number one, Frith, was standing at the side of his seated boss. Frith was over six foot, around thirty heavily tattooed; many of the tattoos were trying to hide the various scars from his violent life.

"Gentleman, I am so glad to see you. N.Y.'s finest are always welcome," Carnello stood to shake their hands over the table. Mercer and Freemond ignored the shake; Freemond sat in a chair opposite Carnello.

Mercer stayed standing, "You asked to see us?"

"Mr Carnello, you lost your manners?" Carnello stated.

Freemond looked at Carnello. "No, you asked to see us?" He supported his partner.

Carnello rose and walked to a bar by the side of the desk. "A drink gentleman?"

"Not while we are on duty."

Carnello looked at Mercer. "Detective Mercer, right. You go by the book I see."

"I try."

"I don't, so what is it *Mr* Carnello?" Freemond over empathised the Mr.

"Ok. It appears that some part time freelance workers for my business have been murdered. I am a little concerned that it could affect my business."

"Workers, you mean hoodlums?"

"Mercer, Mr Carnello is being nice to you, show some respect!"

Mercer eyed his tormentor. "And if I don't, what would you do, strike a police officer, Frith?"

Frith moved towards Mercer, eyes glaring. "You are on my patch here, cop, your rules won't protect you!"

Frith was in Mercer's face; Mercer pounced, pushing Frith against a wall. "Threatening a police officer should do it!" Frith went to respond, and then laughed, three guns were at Mercers head. The room went silent.

"Eh, guys please are you not forgetting I pay you and you are supposed to be protecting me!"

The heavies and Mercer turned to see Freemond now standing, gun at Carnello's head. "Let my partner go. Merce let the punk go." The heavies looked at each other, Frith nodded, the guns were holstered. Mercer gave Frith his toughest look and released him before returning to sit on the edge of Carnello's desk.

"Thank you. Detective Freemond, if you leave that gun at my head any longer I will go for a police brutality case!" Carnello gave a smirk; Freemond lowered but did not holster his weapon. "You two have got it all wrong. I'm a pillar of the community, a property magnet. Hell, I even support the policeman's ball and the children's homes," Carnello said, not quite convincingly. Sat back at his desk he added, "Look, whatever is going on does not help any of us. My workers are being killed; their families and my….competitors are getting edgy. I was speaking to…someone high up and he thinks that a lot of businesses falling out is not good for the city. So working together is key." Mercer gave Freemond a quizzical look.

Carnello continued, "Under your fat arse, Detective Mercer, is a file. In it are some details of my unfortunate part time employees that may be of use to you. I see helping you get the punk doing this as a corporate and civic duty."

Mercer stood from the table, grabbed the file and walked to the door followed by Freemond, who added, "We'll be in touch," as they left.

Sat at the coffee shop opposite the Carnello building Freemond spoke first. "Why the fuck did you go for Frith, are you mad?"

"Sorry, he was in my face. I thought he was going to head butt me. Self defence."

"You kidding? Come on, even Frith would not do that in front of people and in Carnello's office."

"You pulled the gun."

"Oh shit. God, I must be the only man to put a gun to Carnello's head and live."

"For now at least."

"That's not funny!"

"Wait, look, they are leaving."

Freemond looked out the window as Mercer was. Carnello was out first and into a limo with a couple of heavies, the limo moved off. Frith followed but got into a flash Merc which U-turned in front of the watching cops before moving off.

"Flash car, and sexy looking blonde. Crime does pay."

"We are in the wrong job…hold on…I need to answer a text," Mercer pushed some buttons on his cell. "So, what did you make of the meeting, Ray?"

"It is clear if Carnello wants our help he either cannot trust his own people or they don't have a clue." Freemond thought for a while, "Let's say Carnello fell out with Frith. It would be hard to find anyone to turn a gun on Frith. He is one scary mother fuck. However, bring in a professional, put him off the scent then, wham!"

"Wow, I wouldn't rule anything out, but it's a bit too early to make assumptions."

"Maybe, Frith is the key, he is too quiet. No revenge, no reports of busted heads. They are all confused, not rattled."

Mercer thought, "Maybe, it is weird. Let's get back to the station. I'm sure the captain will be happy to see us alive."

Mercer was wrong; as they entered the squad room it was clear the captain was out for the afternoon. Mercer poured the coffees and sat at his desk and read the Carnello file. Freemond sat opposite and made some calls and updated on the forensic side. "Anything?" Freemond asked as he returned to his desk.

"No, not really. Some history on the three vics but nothing that ties them together, apart from the Carnello tie. Has some interesting details of military trained part time workers."

"Oh, read it some more and let me know. Lisa asked if you wanted a meal tonight?"

"Oh, no, not at that plush place. I don't feel like it."

"No, her place, something simple. What am I doing? I'm not a dating agency."

"Good, you would be crap at it."

"Not really, I already said yes for you. 6:30 at hers, enjoy."

Mercer read the rest of the file and either noted or removed some parts. "I'll take some home and read it later. See you in the morning, Ray."

Mercer drove to Barretts apartment meeting Barrett at the door. An hour in and Mercer was sitting eating homemade pasta. He had to admit it was the best food he had had for some time. "I'll wash up?"

"No, sit down pick some music, I will fill the dishwasher."

Mercer sat on the couch and selected a song through the Wi-Fi; Lisa joined him some five minutes later with a couple of glasses of wine.

"No, let me start," Mercer said. "You always want me to talk and yet you are getting over a divorce. Nearly a year now?"

"Year next week to be precise. James was a mover, Wall Street wiz. I lived the life you know."

"You got this place out of him," Mercer giggled.

"He got the big apartment on Lexington, the cars...oh, and the secretary."

"He must be mad, you are ten times the woman she is."

"Yeah, I forgot you and Tanya met her a few times."

"Tanya didn't like her, but she liked you."

Lisa closed her eyes and thought. "Thank you. We went out in a foursome some times if you recall."

Mercer laughed. "Yeah but I didn't like it much especially in the posh places. He's...what...the youngest barrister in the world? And me a cop."

"I think I know which one of you turned out to be the better," Barrett gave Mercer a look. Mercer shifted uncomfortably in the chair. "Oh, sorry, John." Barrett noted his change in mood.

"So you read?" Mercer changed the subject. Picking up a book entitled Enlightenment: Another Earth, from the side table. "I would have thought you read factual books not fiction, especially Sci-Fi?"

"I do," Barrett pointed to her bookshelf, most being science related or autobiographies. "However I do read fiction, ones about love. That one is more about love, family and friends than Sci-Fi."

Mercer looked at the smiling Barrett, rising he said, "Sorry, I need to go, it's late."

"Sorry!" Barrett said also standing.

Mercer looked at Barrett and gave her a kiss on the cheek. "Look, I like you and…but just not now. I'm not ready." Barrett returned the kiss before Mercer left. Barrett sat back down and read her book.

"How long have the dickheads been with the captain, Ray?"

"Morning John. I've been here twenty minutes and they were in his office already."

"Why didn't you call me? It's always fun when the dickheads are here!" Lisa shouted with a mischievous smile on her face.

"Morning Lisa, take a seat, I'm sure we will know shortly."

The Dickheads, were Internal Affairs officers Richard Jenks and Tom Head, an unfortunate name pairing. They were clearly in discussion with captain Ward; it was quite heated going by the arm movements. The captain opened his door. "You two, I mean three, come in!"

The three colleagues entered the office, closing the door behind them—none acknowledged the dickheads. "You all know each other. Give us an update on the case!" The captain ordered.

"No real change Captain. Carnello's info has some interesting bits but nothing to take us forward. What has it to do with the dickheads?" Mercer did not care what they thought.

"Captain Ward, you cannot let him speak like that to us!" Jenks retorted.

"Mercer, have a civil tongue. His name is Dick…I mean, Officer Jenks." Barrett giggled, she knew the captain had meant the name error.

"Captain Ward. You are supposed to set the example!" Head stated.

"And you do?" With this Freemond stood in front of the two internal affair officers. Virtually in their faces he added, "At least we only take our pay from the state."

Both Jenks and Head went to respond, but noting Barrett pointing at the window, turned to look out into the general office. Every cop in the outer office had stood and was looking at them into the office.

Freemond said slowly, "Some twenty colleagues working their butts off for the good of the community on state pay out there. Maybe we should have that argument."

The room went silent. Captain Ward spoke. "Detective Freemond, your accusations are unfounded. Enough."

Freemond nodded his head and moved away from the two unpopular officers. The captain continued, "Jenks and Head, I do not expect you to react, drop it, otherwise I will make it my duty to listen to the rumours and feel of my team."

Jenks looked at Head, "Captain, any suggestions or thoughts you have are scandalous and untrue. But we will over look your officer's comments once you let us do our job."

Captain Ward nodded his head, "I.A. are here to overview the case, you will update them on everything."

"Of course, Captain. We will give them the files when the case is solved and they can review as normal."

"Mercer, I did not say review. I said overview, which means they will be involved in the live investigation." The captain ignored his subordinate's frowns and continued. "You will share everything you have so far and discuss your thoughts with them. Any petty squabbles and I will deal with them, regardless of who or which department. Am I clear?"

All five officers present replied, "Yes sir!"

"Then get on with it, go, but Freemond stay!"

Freemond watched as the others left, the dickheads were at Mercer's desk with him, Barrett had gone to her lab. "Pulling a gun on Carnello is not a good move Ray."

"You do have big ears, Captain."

The captain smiled, "Watch your back and Mercer's. I hear he went for Frith, also stupid."

"You know there is history there. Remember a few years back; he was the last cop to have Frith arrested. Tanya was a junior lawyer then on the prosecution side and all was going well, then Carnello pulled strings. Bent public servants, like those two got involved and the scumbag walked."

"Mercer is not the last or only cop to have nearly got Frith, hell, you have a couple of times."

"Yeah, that robbery some time back I'm still convinced Frith was one of the dirt bags in the mask. I should have shot to kill that day."

"Look, Ray, all is not fair but we turn up and do our job every day and catch more than we lose. I don't like it but Carnello is on our side, those goons are here on his behalf but seriously want to capture the son of a bitch."

"It pains me to say this but you are right. You know my gut feel is Carnello and Frith have fallen out, maybe a power struggle?"

The captain thought, "Would explain why everything is so clinical. If it were another gang we would have war on the streets, which the mayor and D.A. do not want. Do your job, you guys will get him."

Freemond left the captain's office and spent the day updating the dickheads who spent their time between Mercer, Freemond and the forensics lab. 5pm came and they left, Mercer and Freemond were happy to go home.

The next morning, Mercer entered the squad room, acknowledged a few good mornings then stopped in his tracks, Head was in his chair. Jenks was sat at Freemond's desk. "I don't have enough sanitiser for your fat arse, get out of my chair!"

Head looked up, thought better of saying something then moved to another chair. Jenks was given the same greeting from Freemond with the same outcome some five minutes later.

"We want to see the scenes of the crime. Mercer, you were at the first one so I will go with you. Head will go to the other scene with you, Freemond."

"Both scenes have been tidied up, what is the point?" Freemond objected.

"We need to feel it, plus there may be people around we can speak to."

No more was said and Mercer found himself showing Jenks around the old dockyard. Watching Jenks work, even though the scene was clear and open to the public, Mercer was impressed by Jenk's attention to detail. Taking in the surroundings and noting possible witness accounts, Jenks was studious.

"How long have you been back, John?"

"About half hour, Ray, how did it go?"

Ray chuckled, "I told the tramp Head was a Vietcong sympathiser. Boy did he get some jip!"

Mercer laughed, "Shame though, I thought the tramp would have been at the mission."

"He was, I took Jenks there just to wind him up."

"You so and so. Anything come out?"

"No, you guys?"

"No, although Jenks was good I hate to say."

"He has to be, watching his arse everyday you have to be careful." Both cops were in hysterics.

"What's so funny?" Barrett had joined them.

"Nothing Lisa." Barrett could tell this was a lie from Mercer.

Captain Ward came out of the conference room where he had been with the dickheads. "You two, looks like a good day…they said you were helpful…"

"Thanks Captain."

"Let me finish, Ray. They said John was helpful. What's the tramp and Vietcong thing all about?"

Barrett fell in and laughed, Mercer doubled up and Freemond looked away. The captain continued, "Anyway, for your sins the dicks want a day on their own tomorrow just to think. That means you two need to keep out of the way. Unless, of course, you have something else to work on?"

"Day off Captain, paid. I'm up for that," Freemond was thinking of time with his grandchild.

"No Ray. I have a stakeout in robbery tomorrow evening, an extra couple of guns will be of use."

"No Captain, robbery, that's not us," Mercer protested.

"A Friday evening too!" Freemond added.

The captain chuckled, "Robbery is not below you. Hell today's robber is tomorrow's killer. Anyway I have decided, go home but don't expect to work until the afternoon, get here about 3pm. Have a long breakfast guys."

With that the captain left. Mercer looked at the two dickheads in the conference room then addressed Freemond. "They aren't taking the case off us?"

"No, doubt it," Ray replied. "Maybe they do just need some time alone. Look seeing the grandchild in the morning is good for me so I'm up for it."

"Ok. What about meeting at Demis' for brunch, say…1pm…before we get here?"

"That will work, see you tomorrow. Night Lisa," with that Freemond left.

"A quick one at Murph's then? Seeing as though you won't be getting up early?" Barrett asked. Mercer agreed and the two spent an hour or so at Murph's before going home.

Chapter Five

The Robbery

Mercer was first at Demis' and sat himself in their favourite booth. "You really having food man?" Demis asked.

"Yeah, two heart stoppers please," Demis left to get the food.

"Hi Ray. Your watch broken?" Mercer addressed his partner who had just arrived late.

Freemond sat in the booth opposite his partner. "Afternoon John. No, when you get to my age you take things easy."

"Any easier and you will need to pay the state back for lack of hours worked," Mercer joked.

Demis returned with plates of food. Freemond seeing the amount of food exclaimed, "What the! Who ordered that?"

"Hi Ray, John did."

Freemond looked at the giggling Mercer. "Everything on that plate is against doctor's orders. Wait, why are there three?"

"Hey man, it's early and Sondra's got the till so you guys are treating me," Demis sat down and tucked in. All three made some small talk about football before Mercer got to the point.

"So what's the word on the street?"

"Real strange guys, too quiet," Demis finished off his third sausage. "Frith was here last night for a few drinks with his guys. I listened, indeed he spoke to me as well."

"What did he say?" Freemond was intrigued.

"Nothing really, but the guy is spooked. They think it is another gang taking out their guys, they are obviously trying to keep it hidden."

"Hidden?"

"You know, not so obvious as to cause a war."

Mercer finished his plate, "That is unusual, all the gangs seem to be happy to show their strength. Any idea which other gang?"

"The Ramones maybe. Jeff Ramone has a lot of military ties. Maybe revenge for their guy that was toasted a few months back."

Freemond said, "Wait, the guy found burnt to death a few weeks ago on the west side was one of Ramone's. Why didn't you tell us?"

"It wasn't your case. You didn't ask me."

"So tell us now?"

Demis fidgeted and looked very uncomfortable. Mercer asked, "Demis, come on buddy, our case or not you should tell us?"

"Guys, let's say a certain gangland lieutenant had a B.B.Q., not many people would tell on him...even the ones who could consider police protection."

"You're not scared of Frith?"

"Wash your mouth out, Ray, who said Frith? Not me!"

"Ok, we get it, but is it revenge? The vic' was a nobody, right?"

"Ramone's second cousin, illegitimate, of course, so no one knows, oops."

"A possibility but Ramone would have just shot up one of Carnello's joints. Subtle is not his style."

"I'm just putting it out there, Ray."

"Have you heard Rays theory, Carnello is after Frith?"

Demis thought again, "Maybe. The murderer is a pro but if you go through all that to get Frith why not just get him first?"

Freemond nodded in agreement, "Let's go, John. Oh, your bill!"

Arriving at the station Mercer and Freemond went straight to the briefing room, having been beckoned by Captain Ward. On entering the room Mercer froze before acknowledging the lead cop, Detective Moore. Moore gave the briefing, pointing to the picture already on the white board. After an hour of planning Moore added, "So to sum up: Weebber and I at the front door; Casey and Stone the rear left of the alley; Freemond and Merce at the rear right of the alley. Let's get suited and out of here!"

A couple of hours later and Mercer was in the car with Freemond, "8pm and nothing, Ray, this is a wild goose chase."

"Shut up and drink your coffee. Easy money and overtime soon."

Mercer finished off his second coffee of the evening. It was dark and raining outside, their stake out was not obvious even though it was fairly busy around the arcade they were watching. "Good place to launder money with all those coin machines. My guess, there's a fair wedge in there to take. Anyway, what's up with you and Moore?" Mercer ignored his partner. "Come on John, you still brooding. Look, how many times have I told you? Moore could have done no more in your wife's case." Mercer continued to ignore Freemond. "Look it was a hit and run drunk driver, he shot himself a few days later, case closed."

Mercer responded with an edge to his voice, "Really, well maybe Moore could have found the son of a bitch earlier. I could have found out why, then saved him the bother and shot him."

"And where would that have got you? John, sorry, you are being too hard on Moore."

There was a loud crackle on the radio, "Shit, they were already in there, out at the front we're taking fire!" Came through the crackle, shots could be heard in the background.

"That's Moore, move it John!"

Mercer put the car in drive, checked his mirror and hit the throttle; Freemond put the siren on the roof. As the car spun around the corner it was hit by bullets, Mercer swerved and smashed into the car opposite. Even though the airbag had deployed Mercer was out of the door quickly and firing at the robbers, all-hiding behind cars on the opposite side of the road. The third police car screeched to a halt on the pavement opposite, both cops jumped out with weapons drawn and shooting.

"Shoot some fuck, John. I can't get up!" Freemond was leaning across the front seats, bullets flying through the smashed door window closest to the robbers. Mercer ducked then stood tall…two shots and a robber hit the deck. "Now!"

With that Freemond kicked his door open, jumped out and hit the floor. Guns blazing, another robber hit the deck. Casey and Stone saw to the other two culprits, police issue shot guns came in handy, Weebber had taken the robber's van's wheels out earlier. "Officer down!"

Mercer's heart fell, "Ray, check the crooks with Stone!" Freemond approached the van, Stone and Casey joined him. Mercer went to his left, it was Weebber calling. Moore was laying on the floor in agony.

"Is he hit? I'll call an ambulance!"

"No, you fuck, the god damn car hit me when you hit it!" Moore screamed in agony at Mercer.

"Oh, shit, sorry, Moore, you ok?"

"Do I look ok? For Christ sake who needs criminals when you're about!"

Half hour later and all was quiet at the scene. Moore had been taken to hospital with a suspected broken leg and ribs. Forensics was already checking the two dead robbers, the other two, injured with shot wounds, already in cuffs on the way to the hospital. Captain Ward arrived. "Do you know how angry I am for being called out on a Friday night? At least the damn rain has stopped. What happened? It sounded like a gunfight at the OK corral!"

"Captain, those guys were armed heavier than we were briefed, we had no choice." Freemond stood his ground.

"The goddamn place is busy, thank god there were no civilians injured otherwise I'd be busting your badges!" The captain was still angry.

"We were shot at, Captain, fuck your evening!" Mercer walked off.

"Don't Captain, leave him. We know you don't mean it. He's pissed because he hurt Moore that's all."

"I know Ray, that's why I'm here, an officer hurt. You guys did good, sorry."

Freemond nodded and went to his partner sitting on a shop window ledge. "Come on Murphs will still be open, the drinks are on the captain. Well, he's paying when I get the money back tomorrow. Mercer smiled and joined Freemond, Casey and Stone for a nightcap at Murphy's.

Mercer slept most of Saturday but managed to catch a late game with Murphy before burying himself in old videos on the Sunday. Freemond had a quiet weekend with his family. Barrett kept picking up her mobile to call Mercer at least twenty times over the weekend, but stopped before pushing the last digit every time.

"Morning Merce, I'm sorry," the captain was genuinely apologetic as he stood at Mercers desk.

"Morning Captain. No problem Friday was shit. Anyway you will be sorry when Ray gives you the drinks bill." The captain smiled, gave Mercer a pat on the back then went to his office.

"Morning John, good job Friday. I hear you went to the game with Murph Saturday night?"

"Hi Lisa, yes, it was good although we lost."

"I so wanted to call you," Barrett said hesitantly.

"Yeah that would have been nice, you should have," Mercer smiled.

"Maybe that plush meal one evening?"

"Definitely. Believe it has to be a week day for the voucher…book it."

Barrett left the squad room with a smile on her face, passing Freemond on the way out. Upon entering Freemond asked, "Someone's happy, news about the case?"

"Morning, Ray. No, she's got a date. She is booking that flash restaurant for her and I"

Freemond smiled at his partner, "Way to go. Way to go. I need to see the captain."

Freemond went into the captain's office, Mercer watched from his desk. All looked good until Freemond pulled out what was obviously the bar bill for Friday night's drinks. There was an obvious expletive or two before Freemond came out smirking.

Sitting opposite each other the partners chatted, going over the case notes. Twenty minutes in the captain came out of the office and announced, "I'm off to the mayor's office. Oh and the bank, on the way back to get a second mortgage!" The whole squad room laughed as Captain Ward exited.

"He will pay. The shots at the end were a bit much. Hell I didn't see much of Saturday and you went to a game."

"I know. Every time a point was scored the buzzer went. Do you know how many points are in an ice hockey game? My head ached all of Sunday!" Mercer threw an aspirin in his coffee cup for theatrics, again most around laughed.

"No dickheads, hopefully they got lost!" Freemond noted the obvious.

An hour or so later and the dickheads arrived, calling a debrief in the conference room. Barrett joined her colleagues. Captain Ward turned up just in time as the dickheads were leaving at the end of the meeting.

"What did they say?" the captain asked.

"They are happy with how things are going. They can see virtually the total lack of evidence or intel is not taking us any further so they will leave us to it. Obviously we need to email them updates," Mercer filled the captain in.

"Wow, not surprised you maybe a drunken so and so but you can do your job!"

"A couple of the cell phones from Gonzalez and Timo have some known numbers. Unusual as they are normally all burn phones and dumped when we catch one. John and Ray have the details maybe worth picking away at the troops. Someone may talk."

"It can wait until tomorrow but do it."

Tuesday was hard; Freemond and Mercer visited four Carnello minions. Trying good cop/bad cop they fished for information. It was clear either no one knew anything or was prepared to say if they did. By late afternoon and they were talking to their fifth contact.

"Look man, just because some dead guys had my number in their cell don't mean I have anything to do with them," Frino protested.

"Come on Frino, we weren't born yesterday. A couple of days before their murder they called you ten times."

"They must have misdialled, Detective Freemond, sir."

"That won't work, maybe we should take you to your place and search it. If you have been so sloppy with your cell then maybe we might find something of interest there." Frino froze, Freemond thought he had got him until he realised a car had drawn up beside them. Two heavies got out the front, Frith from the back. "Keep calm John, this is not the place to try it. We are in the hood on their turf."

"What are you pigs doing on my streets?"

Mercer stood tall, "Our streets, since when were you elected?"

Frith stopped a few feet from Mercer and looked him up and down. "Why you bothering my friends?"

"None of your business." Mercer and Frith were eying each other.

"Let's all calm down," Freemond walked between them. "We are helping as per Carnello's wishes. You were there when he asked us."

Frith circled for a while, his eyes piercing but lost, Freemond felt scared. "So what have you got?"

Freemond gave a sigh, "Sorry, nothing yet but we are hoping your boys could help."

Frith continued to move from side to side, Mercer watching his every move. "If they knew anything I would know." Frith looked at Frino. Frino cowered.

"Then what do you know?" Mercer asked with gritted teeth. Freemond put his hand near his holstered weapon.

"Getting trigger happy in your old age detective? How is the grandchild?" Freemond used all his inner strength to not pull his weapon.

It was Mercer's turn to play the good guy. "You are right, Frith. If you knew anything and Carnello has asked you to help then I'm sure you would tell us. Let's go, Ray."

With that Mercer moved Freemond away to their car, they got in and Mercer drove off. Stopping near some greenery some miles from the hood, Freemond got out first, taking his anger out on a tree by punching it. "He threatened my grandchild."

"I know buddy. How you didn't pull your gun amazes me but it was the right thing to do."

"I will kill him for that, he has crossed the line!"

"You're a cop, Ray, and a good one at that. He will slip up one day and we will get him." Mercer drove Freemond home and took up Gloria's offer of a meal. Meal eaten and all three sat on the small balcony. "Great food as usual, Gloria."

"Thanks John, it is good to have praise," Gloria looked at her husband, he had been relatively quiet all evening. "Ray, darling. It is rude not to talk to guests!"

"Sorry dear, I think I have a headache. Catch you tomorrow, John, I'm going to bed," with that Freemond left and went to bed.

"What is up with my Ray?"

Mercer thought, "Nothing, Gloria, the case is getting to him. It is so frustrating… three murders and nothing to go on."

"Are you sure, it seems deeper than that?"

"We had a bad day, all round the hood. It's enough to bring anyone down."

Gloria looked at Mercer, "You're a good boy, I'm sure you would not lie to me. How is your mother, I heard you saw her the other day?"

"She is good. Physically very little wrong with her, but you know her mind goes all over the place."

"I will visit her again, maybe the weekend, is that ok?"

"Yes, of course, she loves you and Ray."

"And you, how are you?" Mercer could not stop a tear in his eye, whether it was the strains of the day or him feeling comfortable with Gloria he did not know.

"It's hard, Gloria. Everyday I want to hear the call for breakfast or…" Mercer was nearly fully crying, "the laugh of my baby."

Gloria moved next to Mercer and gave him a hug. "I am so sorry, John, there is nothing we have or could say to change things. But we are here for you."

Mercer gave Gloria a hug back, "I know, friends like you, Ray and Lisa make it easier." Gloria let Mercer cry it out, his head on her shoulder. A short time later Mercer thanked his friend and went home.

Chapter Six

Noting NY's Finest

Freemond was later than usual this morning; the captain picked it up this time. Walking out of his office to Freemond's desk he said, "Ray, it is noticeable now, what's the problem?"

"Sorry Captain, I got in to see my doctor. Nothing bad, probably just age."

Mercer looked at his buddy, he was probably the fittest man for his age he had ever known. "Hey buddy, is it something serious, on-going?"

"No, I think it's in my head. Years at this game and now working with the enemy—it's not right. I'll get the coffee," with that Freemond went to the coffee machine.

"You know him John, is he telling the truth?"

"I'm not aware of any health issues he has. I was with Gloria only last night and she seemed worried."

"How is she?"

"Oh, she is great. Looking after the grandchild has given her a second youth."

The captain smiled, "Keep an eye on him buddy and I may persuade him to see one of our docs. Here come the dickheads."

All the case cops gathered around the case board. Head was leading the questions; although the atmosphere was cold at least all was trying to work together.

With the meeting over and the dickheads gone, Freemond and Mercer sat at their desks, Barrett sitting on Mercer's. "Good news that the dickheads for all their day on their own have found no more than us," Freemond was being defensive about his investigation skills.

"Not really, if there were a hole or we missed something I really would have liked them to have found it. This will get messy, Ray, I see a gangland war coming," Mercer was being more pragmatic.

"So they all shoot each other, saves us paperwork in arresting them and state money on jail costs."

"Ray, you can't mean that!"

"I was joking, Lisa."

Barrett left for her lab, Mercer and Freemond studied the evidence again. A couple of hours later Freemond had had enough of the office. "Let's get out, Ray. We can visit Moore at the hospital."

"Ok, we can count it as police time." With that they both left for the hospital. Moore was on the eighth floor and in a private room, leg in plaster and traction already.

"Keep that fumbling asshole away from my bed." Moore shouted as Mercer and Freemond entered his room.

"I'm sorry, ok? There were bullets everywhere, where the fuck was your, *'they are small time, they won't have many weapons or shoot back'* theory?"

"Ok, ok, we are even!" Moore had to give in.

The three cops passed small talk, and more important, for Freemond, was the working day was almost up. Walking back to their car Mercer received a call. "We are in tonight at 6pm, come and pick me up!" An excited Barrett was shouting down the cell.

"In where?"

"Sauce and Food, the plush restaurant, I got a booking. Come on, it's once in a lifetime!"

"What now? Tonight? That's only a couple of hours from now. I need to change!"

"You always wear a jacket and trousers, John. Besides early evening is less formal in the week so please?"

"Ok, it's been an easy day really. I'll drop Ray home and come and pick you up." Mercer ended the call.

Freemond spoke, "I wish I was twenty odd years younger, a hot lady and a nice restaurant."

"You can take her then if you like. I think Gloria is lovely too!" Mercer replied with a laugh.

"You are right, I am a lucky man. Tell me what it is like as we have an anniversary in a couple of months so maybe Gloria can get her glad rags out."

Freemond dropped off, Mercer arrived in the station car park. Barrett skipped towards the car; wearing a nice short black dress and looking good. "You didn't work in that dress, did you?"

Barrett laughed and sat in the passenger seat. "No, but I have it in the locker just in case. *But, wow, you look good, Lisa* would have been nice."

Mercer did not respond and drove to the restaurant. Walking up to the door, opened by a doorman, the two entered. Mercer looked around, it was plush, and he lost count of how many chandeliers he could see.

"Good evening, may I have your reservation name please?"

Mercer, although suited, felt he was a little out of place, his thoughts being elsewhere, he slightly tripped over his own feet whilst trying to get closer to the man at the reservation pedestal.

"Oops, let me," The receptionist was already helping Mercer to straighten; Mercer caught the receptionist clocking his gun.

"Thank you, I am a cop," Mercer flashed his badge.

"Detective Mercer, I mean Mercer is the booking name."

"Barrett was laughing at Mercer's stumble, "Barrett, I booked it."

"Oh, police officers. Wait here just for a moment," The receptionist went off.

"If he throws us out for being cops or the state of my suit I will check their kitchen for something to close them down," Mercer said quietly.

"Detective Barrett and friend, welcome to the Sauce and Food. I am the manager Mr Court. Please follow me." Court led the two cops to a table that was on a raised platform looking down over the large fancy fish tank and the rest of the restaurant. There were ten tables on the raised area and six were taken.

"One of our best tables," Court said. "This is Wyonna, who will wait on you this evening." Wyonna smiled as she and Court helped Mercer and Barrett get seated comfortably. Court moved to Barrett and whispered something in her ear before leaving with a, "I will check on you a little later but please, enjoy."

Wyonna took their drinks order first; Mercer was alone at the table with Barrett. "Did he say something about my clothes or fall?"

Barrett laughed but said quietly, "No, he did not. He said that the owners had total respect for the police and therefore, our meal tonight and drinks would be free."

"Wow, you are kidding?"

"No, I am not. Frankly seeing the prices of the drinks I am glad—this place is not for our pay scale."

"That's why I ordered a beer."

"Mine was a bottle of wine not a glass."

Two courses in and the evening was going well, Wyonna could not do enough for them. Although the drinks were free, Mercer and Barrett were being sensible, if two bottles of the best white could be deemed sensible.

"Your dessert is on its way, may I be seated?"

"Yes, of course, Mr Court, please do," Barrett was still trying her posh voice.

Court pulled up a chair and sat down. "Our owner, Mr Carmichael, owned a restaurant at the bottom of the twin towers. It was in the terror attack; we lost colleagues, including a highly gifted chef. Mr Carmichael was not in the restaurant at the time but was on the approach to it and witnessed the atrocity. He also witnessed the bravery and tenacity of the supporting ambulance, fire and police staff. He saw the *when there is a danger the public run away, our services run to it* attitude with his own eyes." Court paused, "It has taken this many years to open a new restaurant here in New York, Washington is our main area of operation. Mr Carmichael was considering calling this place Heroes, but sadly the brand name simply around our special sauces had to stay. Anyway we will welcome all our heroes of the services as much as we can. That is why we marketed the discount voucher to the service's H.R. You are the first two so we are happy to provide your meal and drinks free. Sadly we may not be able to do this for your colleagues going forward, but with the discount voucher and my word that we will try to look after you, please get my message out."

Mercer and Barrett could not help but a small tear. Barrett spoke, "Oh, Mr Court, that is so lovely. Tell Mr Carmichael and indeed your staff that the N.Y.P.D. will be advised and if you need us we will be there."

Court raised, replaced his chair and left with a simple thank you.

Dessert eaten, the biggest chocolate and ice cream mix they had ever seen, Mercer and Barrett were outside. Mercer called a Taxi, "My place first the traffic is easier that way?" Mercer asked Barrett. Yes being the reply the Taxi moved off.

As they entered Mercers apartment main entrance, Barrett said, "That was unbelievable, I am going to bust out of this dress!"

Mercer was relaxed, happier then he had been for some time, "Maybe I could help you out of it?"

Taking the lift to Mercer's apartment, they stood in the open doorway and quickly embracing each other. Frenzied kisses first Barrett took a few steps into the room and turned. Mercer closed the door and moved towards her and unzipped her dress, which fell to the floor. Barrett put her semi naked body against Mercer's. They kissed further, Mercer moving them towards a wall. Not been able to go any further Mercer stopped as Barrett ripped his shirt off. Mercer put his chest against hers and the kissing continued. Barrett moved to kissing his neck then his shoulder. Barrett was getting warm, and then froze as Mercer pulled back. Without saying anything he had pulled his top back on and sat on the couch. Barrett did not know where to look so walked to her dress and pulled it back on. Although frustrated Barrett looked down at Mercer, "I am sorry John I misread the signals, although they were very positive signals."

Mercer mumbled. "I'm sorry," but did not look up at Barrett.

Barrett looked up, catching something out of her eye as she looked at the wall where they had just been groping—a picture of Tanya was where her head would have been. *Oh no!* She thought, he must have seen it whilst embracing. "It's ok, John, I understand. Shall I get a drink or maybe go?"

Again Mercer did not look up but said, "I'm sorry, too many memories. Not here, please go."

Barrett said no more, she fully understood so left.

Chapter Seven

Revenge

Whilst Mercer and Barrett enjoyed the comfort of the flash restaurant, on the other side of the city a small Italian restaurant was going about its business. For a Thursday evening Romero, the owner, was quite happy, ten tables filled and food and alcohol being sold. As he went to serve one table he noticed the door open, two heavies came in first with weapons drawn, this told him it was not going to be good.

"Stay still everyone!" The first heavy shouted whilst holding his machine gun high and waving it at all in general. There was a scream from one table, "Shut up bitch! Anyone else and we shoot!" As the first two heavies got further into the restaurant, Frith was behind them followed by two, more heavily armed, heavies. One heavy closed the door behind them, turning the closed sign and pulling the window blind down. Frith stopped; his empty glaze scoured the room. Two more heavies came from the rear kitchen door.

"All clear, boss!" Another armed heavy shouted to Frith.

Romero went to address Frith, "Mr Frith, please, can I do anything for you?" Frith looked at the owner, pushed him aside and walked to a table where two men sat; Ex Sergeant Dobrovski looked up at Frith, he had never met him but knew of his reputation. Dobrovski was armed, but Frith with two heavies armed looking right at him decided not to act.

"Are you Dobrovski?" Frith questioned.

Dobrovski fidgeted in his chair then replied, "Yes. Can I help you Mr Frith?"

Frith looked at Dobrovski coldly, "Are you armed?"

Dobrovski moved his arm towards his chest, "Yes, but I don't want any trouble." Frith's companion moved his arm too. Frith noted the movement and looked at him. A shotgun barrel was put to Dobrovski's companion's head by one of Frith's heavies.

Frith averted his look back to Dobrovski, "Show me your weapon but be careful!"

Dobrovski started to sweat but slowly pushed his jacket aside to reveal his shoulder holster and weapon. Frith lifted his gun and emptied it into Dobrovski; his two heavies beside him took out Dobrovski's companion.

Romero's heart missed a beat, his other customers were shocked but no one screamed, no one wanted to attract Frith's attention. Frith turned and looked at Romero, "No one saw anything!" Looking around the restaurant he continued, "I know you all, I know your families. Razz! Make sure the C.C.T.V. is broken." One of the heavies at the kitchen door nodded a yes. Frith casually walked out the front door.

"You had a good meal, John?" Freemond asked as his partner walked up to him.

"12:15 in the morning, I was just going to bed then this," Mercer was tired.

"Lisa not with you?" Freemond gave a smirk.

"No, no, she left an hour or so ago."

"Oh, I thought…no, never mind. Jackson, what's the situation?"

Officer Jackson approached the two detectives, "Two dead in Romero's. No one appears to be talking. Bodies are in the restaurant, only staff in the kitchen. Our guys are talking to them. Forensics is on their way."

"Thanks," Freemond said as he and Mercer entered the restaurant. "Unless our perp has changed tact it's not him." Freemond looked at the bullet-ridden bodies.

"A Desert Eagle in that one?" Mercer looked surprised.

"Interesting, let's talk to Romero." The cops moved to the kitchen, six cops and three staff plus Romero were present. "So, what happened, Romero?"

"Hi Mr Freemond. Look I don't know…"

"Come off it, Romero, you have two bodies out there with half an armoury emptied into them!" Mercer pushed.

"We were quiet, trade is bad. I served the two guys then came back here to talk to my chef. We heard the shooting, hid here for a while then looked in. We saw the bodies and called you guys," Romero stated, his eyes were not in tune with his words.

"Bullshit, who was it?" Freemond had seen many liars over the years.

"It's true, Mr Freemond, please ask my staff, they will tell you."

The uniform standing next to Mercer spoke, "That's what they are all saying."

Mercer acknowledged his colleague and turned back to Romero, "Frith maybe? Tell us, we can help."

Romero nearly fainted upon hearing those words, "No. No. No not Frith. We saw no one, honest!"

"You need to tell us Romero, scumbags like Frith need locking up!" Freemond looked into Romero's eyes as he spoke.

Romero broke out in a sweat, "No, I told you we saw nothing."

Mercer, saw the C.C.T.V. cameras, "I'll get our forensic bods to check your C.C.T.V."

"Go ahead, maybe they can fix it. It's been dead for weeks." Romero stated.

Mercer shook his head, "Get all their statements and addresses. We may see you all again so think!" With that he and Freemond went to the main restaurant, forensic had arrived.

"Hi Lisa, have a good night?" Freemond gave Barrett a wink.

"Hi Ray, yes, it would appear John has better manners than you," Barrett giggled. Looking at Mercer she added, "It was a very nice evening, this has ruined it though."

Mercer smirked, "The guy on the left has a Dessert Eagle, please tell me we could be lucky?"

Barrett looked at the bodies, concentrating on the one with the weapon showing in his holster. "Maybe, that would be nice. Both look military from their haircuts. Any witnesses?"

Freemond laughed, "None, the place was empty."

Barrett looked around, "My guess is a quick tidy up before we turned up but the half finished drinks on the counter and food on the floor suggest not."

"Do your stuff Lisa, catch you in the morning," Mercer gave Barrett a wink as he and Freemond left the scene.

"I got four hours sleep at best Captain!" Mercer protested as the captain walked straight up to his desk as he had only just sat down.

"Morning John, when Ray gets here you have a guest in interrogation room five. Ramone. He is in for a minor motoring demeanour…his bike was dirty."

"You wanted him off the streets, Captain?" Freemond threw in as he went to sit.

"Nice for you to join us, Ray! But, yes, I need him off the streets, we had an unknown tip the military bodies are known by him."

"Interesting, any news on the gun?" Mercer wanted to know.

"If you guys stopped drinking and going out with each other maybe some work would get done, on time!" Although the captain said this, his laugh gave it away, he was only jesting.

Mercer chuckled, "I thought you wanted your staff to get on?"

Freemond joined in, "You don't take me to Sauce and Food!"

"Does everyone know? I'm going to do my job," Mercer left for the interrogation room. "I hear the bods were your men?"

Ramone looked at Mercer, "I don't know what you mean. Get me out of this place, a dirty bike, this is a travesty of justice!"

Mercer laughed and sat opposite Ramone, "Sorry, but I'll find anything to keep you here until you give me something."

"You can't do that you mother fuck, where is my brief?"

"You, hiding behind the law? That's funny." Mercer laughed.

Ramone stood up quickly and banged the table, "Fuck you!"

With that the door opened and Freemond entered, "Sit down or I'll shoot you for attacking a cop!"

Ramone sat, composed himself and said, "You threatening me, Freemond. You really are testing my patience."

As Freemond moved into the room further, captain Ward was following. "Try threatening me Ramone. My gang's bigger and better armed than yours!"

Ramone looked up at the captain, "Ok, ok, what do you want? This is silly boss man!"

Freemond sat on the table, the captain paced up and down. "Look Ramone, regardless of what shit you guys get up to, the streets have been quiet for some time. You know how it goes, keep your shit to yourselves and, well, we have better things to do, like parking violations," The captain giggled as he spoke. "Duffy, four coffees now please!" The uniformed officer who had been standing in the corner acknowledged his captain and left. "Move your butt Mercer let me sit." Upon sitting the captain continued, "The military guys, were they yours?"

"No…" Ramone paused, "I know them, yes. Ex military Sergeant Dobrovski and private Milner. You could call them mercenaries, usually abroad."

"You hired them to take Frith out because of what he did to your cousin?" The captain noted Ramone was moving uncomfortably. "Look, we have the cameras and mic off. This is between us; after all once it is just you lot killing each other I'm not concerned. Hell, if I could afford a hit man I would consider taking Frith out." Mercer and Freemond both winced at their captain's words.

The tactic seemed to work, "Captain, if what you say is true then an outside person, not tied to someone, would be a good way to deal with things. I like my present life, as much drugs and pussy as I can get and you guys normally leave me alone."

"So Dobrovski and/or his buddy are our killer?" Freemond was intrigued.

Ramone smiled, "Look, I have a very upset hot aunt and to make her happy maybe, just maybe, Frith having an accident would be a good thing. But, no, I don't think so; even men of Dobrovski's profession have rules. They only do what they are paid to do. No money has changed hands so no deal has been done."

The captain thought, "Hopefully the forensics will tell us differently. I assume Frith or Carnello picked up on Dobrovski before us?"

Ramone laughed, "Oh, Captain, I can give you a *head* start on that one!"

The captain and Freemond laughed, Mercer could not hold back, "What the fuck is going on here. He is virtually admitting he has hired a hit man and suggested Detective Head is bent, which we all know. We need to arrest him for more than a dirty bike!"

"Shut up, John!" The captain acknowledged Duffy as he returned with coffees. "Thanks Duffy, leave us." The captain shared out the coffees and continued, "Ramone, you are here to stop a blood bath. You know I will hold you as long as I can."

Ramone nodded, "I'm not giving you anything concrete."

"I know…" The captain was stopped by a cell message beep. Following the noise he looked at Mercer. Mercer showed the captain the message. The captain continued, "You will stay here a few hours more, my men will look after you then release you. But I need your word you will leave Carnello and Frith alone, we will find the killer."

"Get me a bacon sandwich and it's a deal, boss." Ramone responded.

"I'll get it sorted. John take your partner out and educate him."

Mercer and Freemond needed no more and left for Barrett's lab.

"So Dobrovski's gun is not a match as your text said?"

"Sorry John, no it was not. His colleague had a different make. Unless, of course, he had other weapons. Uniform are at his last known address, some hotel on Broad, as we speak," Barrett filled her colleagues in.

"Damn that suggests our perp is still out there. Someone needs to give us a break," Mercer looked to the sky as he spoke.

"Hey buddy, hold on, who knows? The hotel may show more. Fancy a drive?" Mercer followed his buddy. Having visited the hotel Dobrovski and his colleague were staying at first thoughts there was no evidence to tie them to the killings or even Ramone. Mercers cell beeped again, "Ray, Demis wants to see us but at the bridge, let's go."

Mercer parked the car, unlit siren on the dashboard to stop them getting a ticket then he and Freemond headed onto the Brooklyn Bridge. Walking a short distance they could tell the hooded figure of Demis, whom they approached.

"Afternoon guys," Demis welcomed them.

"Hiding Demis?" Mercer asked.

"It's still daylight, and besides, my place is not the best place today. I enjoy the river air here and can think."

"You're right," Freemond spoke after taking in the air. "What you got buddy?"

"Frith and his gang shot the military guys last night. But you won't get any witnesses. It seems as though he heard Ramone had some paid guns in to take him out."

"We knew that buddy, but thanks for the unofficial confirmation." Freemond responded.

"Are the military guys your killer?"

"No, we don't believe so at this point."

Demis looked around, "Damn. You guys need to do your jobs, as Carnello and gang are now trigger-happy. I have not seen a full out gang war for some time but it is not good. Even civilians like me can get caught up in it."

Mercer looked at Demis, "What's up buddy, you are on edge?"

Demis took in a breath of air, "Nothing, just get this sorted please." Demis then walked off.

"What do you make of that Ray? He is rattled."

"Watch!" Was Freemond's response. Mercer watched and saw Demis get into a limo.

"That's Frith's car," Mercer was a little shocked.

"Yep. Frith knows Demis talks both ways. This meeting was to let us know he did it and he will do it again unless we give him the perp. As he now knows he did not get him."

Mercer took a few steps, "Look, Ray I'm not stupid but this honour amongst thieves thing cuts me."

Freemond looked at his partner and smiled, "Come on John, you know the way things go. We can't lock everyone up."

"Does that not make us as bad as them, even bent like Head and everyone else?"

Mercer's comments cut into Freemond before he replied. "Maybe, but no, there is a big difference between us and them. We have morals, ok we stretch them a bit but the city would not work without an understanding between us and the big guys out there."

"Oh, Ray, it's hard but yes, I understand. We need to get the perp though, right?"

"Yes and soon, before this city explodes.

Chapter Eight

The Kidnap

Returning to the station the captain had called for an update. Barrett smiled at Mercer and started, "On our perps case, nothing further on forensics. Some of the cell data led us to hoodlums as you know. Again, nothing on the case but maybe we have a few troublemakers off the street. Regarding the $50k found in Timo's car, all the notes have been analysed and a few were from some known thefts. Our colleagues are looking at those."

"We are no further either, Captain. I even spoke to Jenks a little earlier and they are as lost as we are."

The captain was surprised at Mercer's comment, noting the collaboration with Internal affairs, "And last night? The mayor and D.A. are chewing my arse."

Barrett replied, "No evidence to tie our two dead soldiers to our perp. Their murder definitely involved multiple weapons and killers. We have the bullets but nothing to tie them to any known guns. Maybe a raid on Carnello's gang would provide the weapons?"

Freemond chuckled, "This is mad, the biggest crime boss in the city with the craziest psycho in tow and apart from last night, there is no bedlam. They must be behind this!"

"I'm beginning to go with Ray on this. Carnello is clearing his gang out."

"Then why would he give you that file, John?"

"Captain, I've been through it a hundred times now and there is nothing. It is all show."

The captain thought, "Yeah I see it now. Carnello is playing us, maybe even laughing at us. What is his end game I wonder?"

A little later Mercer entered Barrett's lab. "Hi John. You ok?"

"I'm sorry about last night Lisa."

"No, no, don't be. I understand."

"Look, there will be the right time and place. I like you."

Barrett gave Mercer a peck on the lips, "When you are ready, I'll be here."

"Thank you. Can I use your P.C. again as you have more open privileges than us. I am going to get a voucher for Ray and Gloria; their anniversary is coming up. Thirty years I think."

"Yes of course. That's lovely, can we go halves on payment?"

"Yes, give me a minute."

Barrett moved to another table to clear up for the evening but could not help but look at her colleague. He was a good man; there was a smile on his face whilst hitting the keyboard (typing was not Mercer's forte). The smile was obviously him thinking of a nice surprise for their friends.

"You take it, maybe wrap it up in some way so as we can give to them," Mercer said as he pulled the printed voucher from the printer.

Taking the voucher Barrett said, "I will. I am at the pictures with Townsend tonight, a girly film. I don't think you would like it?"

"No, no, you are right. Enjoy and I'll see you Monday…maybe Sunday?"

Barrett smiled, "Yes, give me a call tomorrow and we can plan something. I fancy a walk at the seaside or in the woods maybe."

"See you Sunday."

Dowd got out of the car; stretching his legs he took a look around. It was dark and damp; the rain had only just stopped. Resting his big frame against the hood he pulled out a smoke and lit up. Sitting in the car for two hours waiting for his boss was easy money but boring. Enjoying his smoke Dowd did not notice the hooded figure coming towards him until he was up close. "Hey man, out of my space!" Dowd felt a sharp pain in his chest.

The figure supported Dowd's body, moving it further into the alley the car was parked in. Chauffer cap and jacket removed, the figure threw the body into one of the dumpsters.

Taylor Caine fell down the couple of steps leading out of the apartment block, the doorman catching her. "Are you ok, Miss Caine?" He asked as he helped the very drunk woman to her feet.

"Where's my car, he's late...sack him!" Caine slurred her words.

The car pulled up, two minutes late, at just gone 11pm. The doorman did not wait for the driver but opened the door and helped Caine in. Caine went flat over the rear seats. "Take her home Dowd!" Was all the driver needed, as the door shut the car moved off.

"Wake up, Ma'am!"

"Oh my head, Dowdy does!" Caine was not aware of her surroundings. "Move quick I'm going to…" Too late, the car took a mouthful. "Sorry Dowd, you will have to clean that up…" Caine stopped. Now halfway out of the car she saw the figure in front of her was not Dowd. "Who the fuck…" Caine said no more as she was hit and fell unconscious.

Coming around, Caine saw the ceiling; the pain in her jaw was intense. First trying to talk she could not, and then she tried to move her arms, they did not move. Her eyes clearing she looked around. She was in a darkish room but off the floor, she looked down and could see her naked breasts. "Oh no!" She tried to cry out but her broken jaw would not let her. Catching a moving figure, Caine looked down towards her legs. A hooded figure was standing between her naked and tied legs. NO! NO! NO! Caine shouted in her head as she felt the figure enter her. Caine tried to move, tried to yell but the abuse went on. Feeling the figure relax, Caine took a breath, then looked down toward the figure only to see the barrel of a gun.

"John, it's a Saturday afternoon I'm shopping with Gloria," Freemond shouted down the cell.

"Ray, another body on Mason, we think Dowd one of Carnello's men. I'm on my way!"

Freemond needed no more, he made his excuses and was soon pulling up under the police cordon at Mason Avenue. Getting out of the car he could see colleagues everywhere, one, catching his eye pointed to the alley. Freemond entered the alley, he was last again.

"Afternoon John, what's the story?"

"Hi Ray, one body in the dumpster found by a tenant putting her rubbish out this morning. I've had a look I think it's that Dowd guy, he drives for Carnello."

Freemond looked in the dumpster, "Yeah, I'm sure that is him. But he still has his head so it's not our guy?"

"Who knows, but he is a Carnello. We have company."

The dickheads were on the scene. They acknowledged Mercer and Freemond, then checked the dumpster. Jenks froze then turned, "It is Dowd, Frith's driver."

Freemond looked shocked, "Frith's?"

"Yes, he was driving Frith's girl last night, Taylor Caine. She visits her sister in the block over there every other Friday night."

"Then we need to speak to her," Mercer was ready to walk.

Head stopped him, "Don't bother and don't ask me how I know this but Caine his girl has not been seen since last night."

"My turn, guys stop fighting over my body!" Barrett was walking toward the dumpster.

Head reacted first, "Sure Barratt. Jenks and I will see the sister, you guys speak to the doorman and check any C.C.T.V." For once there was no backchat, if Frith's girl was involved in anyway then this could get out of hand. The four cops entered the apartment reception, Jenks and Head went to the lift, Mercer and Freemond to the doorman.

"Are you ok, buddy?" Mercer asked, the doorman was quite a frail old man and clearly looking shocked.

"Yes, the man, over there, is it Dowd?"

"We believe so but it needs confirming, Taylor Caine?"

The doorman looked sad and distraught. "Miss Caine, oh my, Miss Caine. I put her in the limo last night. Where is she now? I heard Stacey, her sister, is upset upstairs."

Before Mercer could respond a man entered, ignoring the Freemond's cries, "Hey buddy, this place is in lock down."

"I'm Frank Caine, I am seeing my sister. Do you guys have anything on Taylor?"

"No, sorry, Mr Caine. Dobbs take Mr Caine up to his sister!" Mercer shouted before turning to address the doorman.

"You put Taylor Caine in the limo, did you see Dowd in the driver's seat?"

"It was dark, I just opened the car door and Miss Caine fell in, drunk. He had a cap on; it was the usual Merc, I don't know. I'm sorry."

Mercer put his hand on the doorman's shoulder, "Look, take a break but we will need you to come to the station and make a statement please."

"Yes, yes. Anything to help Miss Caine."

Mercer pulled out his cell and called the tech team. "Taylor Caine has been abducted in a Merc-limo, I'll text you the plate no., see if you can find it. All Mercs have modern navigation. Also see if you can get a fix on Caine's cell."

Mercer got the plate and cell information off the doorman and text the details. Mercer looked around and asked to access the buildings C.C.T.V. "Look, the Merc has pulled up. Too dark, replay it pulling up."

The security operator replayed the scene of the Merc pulling up outside the apartment. "Not good, you can hardly make the driver out, just uniform and cap. Can we have a copy and any other angles if you have them, please," Freemond requested.

Freemond and Mercer took a walk outside to assess the entrance and surroundings. Mercer's cell rang, "Yes. No but I know where it is we will drive there now. Get a couple of squad cars to meet us there." Mercer looked at Freemond, "Got the location of the Merc's last G.P.S. position albeit 11:15 last night, let's go!"

Both cops jumped into their car and shot off, siren blaring for the short drive. Just as they were about to pull up they received a call. "Uniform on site, no Merc, but Caine's phone just came on line, Lincoln, two blocks up in a play area!" Mercer did not stop but floored the throttle, Freemond calling one of the two stopped squad cars to follow them. Turning the corner Mercer saw a playground in front of them, there appeared to be only kids there. The kids, upon seeing the police car, split, running off. Mercer took after one kid on foot who appeared to have a cell in his hands. Freemond and the two squad car cops were chasing the others. The kid dropped the cell; Mercer left it as he caught the kid a few feet from where it was dropped. "Leave me alone, pig, I did nothing!"

"Hold still!" The kid froze as Mercer held him tight by the shoulder, very tight. "I'm not after you, calm down." Mercer then pushed the kid to walk and led him to the dropped cell. Mercer picked up the glitzy gold coloured IPhone with an evidence bag. "Where did you get this?"

"It's not mine!"

"I know. Where did you get it?"

The kid went quiet; "I'm only thirteen so you need a parent with me."

"Only if I am to arrest you, which is not my intention. Kid, I assure you I am not interested why you have this but I do need to know where you found it?"

The kid thought for a second, looked up and could see three of his friends who were with him being led towards him by policemen. "We found it about half hour ago near some bins round the block. We just charged it with an emergency charger, but it is locked. Please don't arrest me."

"I won't, but you need to show me where. Come on. Freemond get the car, I'll meet you and the others on the main road where the Merc was meant to be!" Mercer's feel was right, as they walked onto the main road the kid showed Mercer where he had found the phone. Under some trash bins by the side of the road where the Merc's G.P.S. was saying it had been last. "You only found it about half hour ago?"

"Yes sir!"

Mercer's solid grip was scaring the kid. "Thank you. Look, go to your friends with the uniforms. They will take your details and call your parents if you need them."

"You think that's Caine's?" Ray was approaching Mercer.

"Yes. I can't open it but I can turn it on and off and see if Tech pick it up." Mercer called the tech team, by turning the cell off then on they were able to confirm it was Caine's.

"Thoughts John?"

"Guess the perp stopped the Merc here, threw the cell out and somehow deactivated the cars GPS." Within fifteen minutes more police and forensics were on the scene, a car fuse found and Mercer's guess was supported.

Uniform had started going door-to-door enquiries with the few businesses and houses opposite the bins; one uniform called Freemond and Mercer over to a kebab shop to talk to the manager. "You were working last night?" Mercer started.

"Yes, it was quiet both in the shop and on the street."

"Did you see anything around eleven last night on the road?"

"Yes. A little after eleven a limo pulled up, stopped at the side of the road for a minute or so then pulled off."

"What kind of limo, did you see the driver?"

"A big Merc, it was Frith's limo. We all know what cars to avoid in this area. I looked, his chauffeur in the front, clearly had the cap on. I couldn't tell if it was the chauffeur guy."

"Can you describe him?"

"Black I think but, no, sorry, not sure."

"Anyone else in the car?"

"No, seems like the driver only."

"Did you see what he did, like throw anything out of the window?"

"No not really, just stopped, he did seem to move around a bit but I couldn't see from here see if he opened any windows. Definitely didn't open any doors though."

"Direction it was heading?"

"Yeah south."

"Any other cars around or people that may have seen something?"

"No, it was late, dark and wet. I have trouble getting business here when light and sunny at night!" Mercer thanked the shop manager and asked uniform to take a full statement. The kids details were all noted and allowed to go with one of the parents who had turned up, Mercer and Freemond went back to the station.

"Updates?" The captain asked those present.

"No, forensic evidence on the cell, but it is Taylor Caine's. No forensics around the bins, even the fuse removed to fool the G.P.S. was clean. Again, none of use at Dowd's scene, the knife was clean."

"Suggests Dowd knew his attacker if no struggle?"

"Maybe or he was caught unawares, again the knife wound was professional and quick. Oh and no C.C.T.V. of any use, the best is the shape of a driver in a cap, possibly black."

"Jenks?"

"No leads from the Caine family, they hate Carnello and Frith but no obvious or recent threats to Taylor that they are aware of."

"Freemond, something, please?"

Freemond looked a little nervous, "No, sorry, Captain, any ransom demands?"

"If it is our perp I doubt it would be for ransom," Barrett stated.

"We have an A.P.B. out on the limo and Taylor Caine, there is nothing you guys can do tonight. Go home but we have a Sunday work day tomorrow."

Chapter Nine

The Suspect(s)

"Morning Ray, you in on time?"

"Hi John, not sure how you make that out, we were not working today so I thought ten was a good time to get in. How long have the dickheads been in with the captain?"

"About ten minutes."

The captain came out of his office with the dickheads. "I have had a call from Taylor's brother, he wants to see some straight, sorry, I mean local cops so you two need to go. His offices on Park. Then maybe rattle Ramone again?"

"Can we fit church in too Captain," Mercer said with a chuckle as he and Freemond left for Frank Caine's office.

"Thank you for coming here, I needed a break from my sister who is extremely upset. A drink? Coffee of course."

"Yes please two black no sugar," Freemond responded to Frank Caine.

"I hear you two are straight, unlike those two yesterday."

Mercer smirked, "What makes you think that, Mr Caine?"

"Come on I work for Carnello so I have some…views."

"Yeah, we know and would be interested in those views." Freemond pushed.

Caine motioned the two detectives to sit then started. "Look, let me be clear, I work for Carnello's legitimate property business. I am an architect that is why I have this lovely office. I have no dealings with any shady side that Carnello may be into." Caine sat down, "I got this job in the normal way, college trained etc. not knowing anything about Carnello's background. I come from a nice part of town, as does Taylor. We were naive. Anyway over time I picked up on my bosses reputation but my side is fully legit it never really effected me. Then a few years back I brought Taylor to the company Christmas party. Carnello turned up completely out of the blue, with

Frith." Caine gritted his teeth upon speaking Frith's name. "Taylor fell for Frith, what the fuck is it about the bad boys attraction!" Caine banged the table with his fist. "Anyway since then they have become an item and Taylor has all the riches but all the troubles of being a gangster's moll. My other sister, our parents and I frown on this but we cannot change her. We live with it and are hoping Taylor will see sense one day."

Mercer spoke, "I am sorry, Mr Caine. You obviously have no time for Frith."

"That's an understatement!"

"So what do you have to help us? Obviously Taylor's kidnapping is our first priority." Mercer continued the conversation.

"Do you have anymore on Taylor's kidnapping?"

"No, nothing of use as yet, we are following up leads."

"Shit, if something happens to my sister I…"

Freemond interrupted, "We know. Is there anything you can think of to help us? Did Taylor fall out with anyone, or had threats?"

"No. Maybe to do with Frith's shit but no, nothing we are aware of. Look, I will make a deal with you. You find my sister and I will help you infiltrate Carnello and Frith and get them locked up at some point."

Mercer thought, "Mr Caine, that would be of real benefit, you will go up against Carnello and Frith?"

"Yes, I have stood back too long. But my sister first!"

"Thank you Mr Caine, as soon as we have something we will get back to you."

Freemond and Mercer headed towards Ramone's; Ramone hung out regularly at a diner with his biker friends. "Do you think Caine will help us with Carnello?"

"Yes I believe he will, John, however, I am not so sure we will find Taylor alive."

Mercer nodded in agreement with his partner, then steered the car into the diner car park. As usual on a Sunday afternoon it was packed with motorbikes and bikers. Exiting the car the two cops walked to the entrance, being jeered by the varied bikers as they walked. As they stepped inside a big hairy biker stood in front of them. "It's a private party, clear off!"

Mercer flashed his badge, "We have an invite."

"The badge means shit, clear off!"

Mercer eyed the man in front of him, he was a big unit, and maybe best not to upset him he thought. "We are here to see Ramone so move your fat arse out of my way!" Freemond pushed past the man without a care.

"I'm with him!" Mercer added as he followed his partner to a booth near the back of the diner. Again at the booth two heavies stood up, Ramone stayed seated.

"A quiet word Ramone or we will take you to the station again. Oh, by the way I have ten squad cars up the road as back up and a full S.W.A.T. team!" Freemond was pushy.

"Leave us, have a seat my friends," Ramone replied with a smirk.

"This changes the game!" Mercer accused.

"We have a deal. Why would I do this?"

"Come on, your hit man is dead, kidnapping a civilian is not in our deal!"

"I don't know what you are on about."

Freemond raised his voice, "Will another day in the cell help?"

Ramone was agitated and fell for it, "Look, if what you say is true then it would have been dealt with by now, pig!"

"Not your usual style though, you getting soft?"

Ramone stood up, "Get lost pig!" Freemond had gone too far, the sound of a few sirens pulling up outside broke the air. "What is going on?"

"You thought I was joking about back up? So in the spirit of good will, as I am sure neither of us want trouble, we need to talk outside!" Ramone looked at his men, he knew they were armed and would outnumber the cops but an open gun shoot out was of no benefit. "Round the back!"

Ramone, Freemond and Mercer stood together at the back door, Freemond waved to the officers who were standing at their squad cars. Some six cars in total. "Talk, or more will come. We are not interested in anything other than finding the Caine girl."

"I have nothing to do with that. If I were that way inclined then I would probably shake the hand of the guy who 's done it."

Freemond thought, "We have a common enemy and after our talk yesterday I thought we had an understanding."

Ramone looked at Freemond, they had history and although on different sides there was some respect between them. "We do. Look this is not my style. I have respect for women."

"So what do you think now, Carnello taking out his own gang? The soldiers just an unfortunate distraction? Taylor Caine is not a hood, we want her not the perp who is taking out the Carnello gang." Mercer was again surprised by his partner's way, but Taylor Caine was their immediate priority.

"Look Freemond. I am no informant but it is unfortunate when, let's say, normal people, get caught up in business affairs. Whether you take my word for it or not I am telling you I have nothing to do with this."

Freemond looked into Ramones eyes, "I believe you. Let's go Merce."

Monday morning came and Mercer got into his car for the drive to work. Turning on the radio the local station announced, *$1 million dollars, yes 1 million dollars is the reward to anyone who provides details on the whereabouts of socialite Taylor Caine…* Although the announcer went on Mercer drove quicker and upon reaching the station he was up with the captain and Barrett.

The captain was astonished, "The idiot. More money than sense that Carnello!"

Barrett responded, "Maybe it will work a million dollars will buy someone, something."

The captain gave Barrett a look, "Our phones have not stopped ringing since the radio and, now, T.V. announcements. We have eighty sightings already, I won't have enough cops to follow them up by noon if this continues!"

"Look Captain, if one turns out the right one it will be useful," Mercer took cover as the empty plastic water cup flew past his head from the captain.

"Not happy today then?" Freemond had entered the room, late again.

"Hi buddy. I do think the captain is right this will just tie up all our resources."

"I know John. Good old fashioned police work, get the coffees Barrett we need to think and look at the evidence." Barrett carried out Freemond's instructions. An hour later and Freemond noticed a commotion, looking at the door he spoke. "Shit fireworks, look who is here!" Mercer turned his head to see the Mayor heading towards the captain's office. The next person to enter the room and follow the mayor was Carnello. Frith stood outside the captain's office.

"My god the mayor and Carnello together that has to be a first," Mercer spoke.

"Carnello and Frith in a police station, I hope we keep them here." Ray chuckled.

Barrett sat on Mercer's desk. Mercer addressed her, "You don't miss a thing, are we bugged?"

"No, just friends." Barrett stated throwing a glance at the desk sergeant. "Getting frenzied in there. And Frith looks cold, frightening to be honest."

"Maybe now's the chance to wind him up. We outnumber him by hundreds at least." Freemond spoke before rising.

"No Ray. No!" Barrett had moved to stop her colleague from going to Frith.

Frith saw the cop's movements and decided to head to them. "My girl, tell me you have found her!"

Barrett replied, "No, I'm sorry, Mr Frith but not yet."

Frith looked at Barrett, "Get off your butts and find my girl!"

Mercer stood. Although he did not like Frith this was not the time or the place. "Look Frith, we have our differences but not on this one. We want to find Taylor too."

Frith's look did not change, but focussed on Mercer, his eyes piercing into Mercer's. "You had better be. The suits in there talk, I don't. Find my girl or I will call war on this department!"

Freemond had had enough, "Frith, you think threatening a whole police department is a good idea?"

As Frith turned to address Freemond, Barrett pushed between them to lower the tension. "Mr Frith, I can assure we are doing all we can. As Merce said we are on the same side. Please have a coffee with me and we can talk. Maybe you have something of use for us. Time is not what Taylor has."

Both Mercer and Freemond were astonished, Frith did not respond but followed Barrett to the coffee machine, and spoke to her. Mercer sat back down, "Oh my god how did Lisa manage that, he is talking to her?"

Freemond also sat, "No idea but if she had not got involved I would have wound him up and you and the others could have shot him." Both cops laughed.

Ten minutes later and the captain's door opened, the mayor, Carnello and Frith left. The captain motioned Freemond and Mercer in, Barrett followed. "The mayor has put extra staff on our call lines, we have cancelled all leave for our boys and we will follow up as many leads as possible."

Before Barrett spoke the dickheads had joined them. "It is no way an internal fight, Carnello would not be so public as this."

Head responded to Barrett, "Frith is pulling the strings here, whether Carnello is the boss or not, Frith scares him. Taylor is pregnant with Frith's baby!"

Everyone in the room hearts shrank. Mercer spoke first, "How long pregnant?"

"Only a month, please don't ask me how I know."

Barrett thought, looked at Mercer and casually held his arm. Mercer looked at Barrett, gave her a smirk and added, "Poor man, no wonder he is so wound up."

Everyone in the room knew Mercer's story, no one spoke for a few minutes. The captain spoke, "Head, here are some names of people who Carnello thinks could be involved. I would suggest you look at the military trained ones first."

"Yes, Captain," Head and Jenks left the room to analyse the list.

"You two look at Caine's background, the brother Caine that is. Carnello has suggested that he may be behind this. The murders are real but he thinks the kidnap is a hoax, all to get at Frith especially with the baby news. They told me in the office before Head blurted it out."

Freemond and Mercer did as they were told, vigorously going through the case notes and computer files. Freemond was the first to find something, "Hey Deano over here!"

An old, uniformed sergeant walked up to Freemond's desk. "What you want Ray?"

"You did the south side years ago, do you remember the Pegasus gang?"

"Yeah." Deano itched his head, "Denzil Olman ran that gang, small petty crime, nothing big."

"A bit of a Fagin, old Denzil." Freemond laughed.

"What has that got to do with this?" Mercer was listening.

"Nothing, I just saw Frith was a member all those years back," Freemond replied.

Deano added, "Yeah, that's right, the little motherfucker was one of Olman's henchmen. Tough fuck even in those days, although he was just a teen. I think I'm the only guy who has ever actually locked him up. Albeit for a minor commotion, hitting a policeman. Me!"

"You should have shot him!" Freemond again was taking no prisoners.

Mercer laughed, "So, where we going with this Ray?"

"Olman is still about, he lives on that run down estate on the south side. If I recall he was an in-guy until Carnello basically moved in and took his gang. He won't have any concerns about spilling the beans on Carnello or even Frith. Worth a conversation."

"A plan for tomorrow then," Mercer stated.

"No, how about today? Look John, I've not told anyone but the captain. I have a doctor's appointment in a half hour so it's on the way. Do the docs then Olman. You coming, I need a lift."

Mercer followed his partner out of the station and into the car, Mercer drove. "You ok, Ray?"

"I'm ok buddy. Just some test results hopefully all will be fine. Age catches us all up you know." Once outside the surgery, as Ray got out the car he spoke, "Look ten twenty minutes then we can go to Olman's. There's a diner just up there, charge me for the coffee."

Mercer nodded a yes and pulled away. Instead of driving direct to the diner Mercer called Freemonds wife. "Are you sure, John? I knew Ray had an appointment but he never mentioned test results?" Gloria said on the cell.

"That's what he said to me, Gloria!"

"Look, I can get a taxi there in five minutes so I will meet him."

"Shall I wait and take you both home?"

"No John, you do your police things, I'll deal with my husband. But thank you."

Chapter Ten

Disturbing Findings

"Officer down! Officer down!" Mercer shouted through his cell before he fell to the floor. His head was spinning but he was not unconscious. The fallen cop did not wait long as within a minute two squad cars came roaring up to him, officers jumping out.

"You ok, Merce?" One uniformed officer was at Mercer's side. Mercer had somehow risen and was sat on a small wall. "I'm ok, but feel shit!"

"Hoolahan. Get the first aid kit, Merce is bleeding!" The uniform spoke again and was shortly joined by a colleague who went about seeing to the bleeding wound on Mercer's head.

"Forget me, he went that way!" Mercer shouted.

The first cop asked, "Who?"

"The guy that hit me, tall, hooded, black!" The cop took off. Mercer added, "Be careful he is dangerous, he's our killer!"

Within minutes the place was full of squad cars, sirens blaring, and an ambulance. The paramedic was seeing to Mercer's wound, as he sat on the wall. An unmarked car pulled up and out jumped the captain with Barrett. Both approached Mercer. Barrett addressed the paramedic, "How is he?"

"He will be fine, the blood is stopping. May get away without stitches but I would prefer him to come to the hospital."

"I'm fine, thank you."

"What are you doing with that?" The captain asked whilst pointing to the floor.

Mercer looked down, a Desert Eagle was on the floor in front of him. "I knocked on Olman's door, just here, behind me. There was no answer although it was ajar, as I entered, gun drawn, I saw Olman. Oh shit, he must be dead." Mercer paused; Barrett gave his hand a grasp for support. "Next I know someone was on me. We fought; I had dropped my gun but managed to push him against the wall. Somehow, I don't know if he went for it or not, but his gun fell to the floor. I felt my head spinning and fell too. I must have picked his gun up not mine. I think I got off one or two shots before he ran out. I chased and fired one here then could not carry on." Mercer froze as he realised the situation he had been in. "Oh my god, it was our perp, I had him in my hands, that is his gun!"

Barrett gave Mercer a hug, "Get in the ambulance, and let us do our bit."

"Wait!" The captain shouted, "If it is our perp what did he look like, which way did he go? By car or on foot?"

"He looked black, but he appeared to have a mask on, hooded dark clothes, my height and build I would say. He took off that way on foot." The captain moved off and gave out his orders, Mercer walked to the ambulance and sat while the paramedic attended to his injury further.

"Hi buddy, you ok?" Freemond was looking into the ambulance.

Mercer smiled, "Hi Ray, how are you?"

"Oh, it's not about me for now, that's later. I hear you nearly whipped or perps butt?"

"Oh, I wish I had. Excuse me, may I get out?" Mercer addressed the paramedic.

"You will survive so yes, but a hospital visit later, right?"

"Yes, of course, thank you." With that Mercer walking towards Olman's house with his buddy.

Barrett met them at the gate. "You were right, blew Olman's head off, you walked straight into it. You can go in and look if you like, I'm dealing with the gun."

Freemond and Mercer walked into the small house, Olman's body was seated in a chair, his head mostly missing. The fallen furniture and blood on the floor were the signs of the struggle. After taking in the scene the two cops went back outside, Mercer sat on the wall where he had earlier.

"He can't be far, strange there was no car." The captain had joined them, "We have officers everywhere, looking at houses but the place is run down and no one wants to know or help."

"Great place to hide a kidnapped woman," Freemond spoke; he was about to find out.

"Captain! Two blocks down one of our guys has seen a limo Merc inside a garage!" A uniform was calling to the captain.

"There cant be any body round here who can afford a Merc. Let's go. Tell no one to approach the house until I say so!" The captain ordered as he, Freemond and Mercer jumped in his car.

"It's been ten minutes Captain, what should we do?" A uniform asked.

"Wait until the S.W.A.T. team are ready," the captain ordered.

Freemond thought this was funny, "Captain we have a small army of our guys here already. It is a small house and Dowd's Merc is in the garage?"

"I know Ray but this guy is military. Who knows, booby-traps maybe? Let the professionals do it first. Donavan, any response to your calls?"

"No Captain!"

"Then go in!"

With that command twenty armed and suited S.W.A.T. team members entered the house. No gunfire, no smoke bombs then finally the S.W.A.T. leader came out of the building's front door. "It is safe Captain, you can go in. But…it's not nice."

Barrett had joined the team and all four entered the house. It was empty, run down with frail curtains pulled on every window. Mercer noticed one S.W.A.T. member walk from the kitchen area, holding his mouth. Within a few steps Mercer knew why. "Oh my god!" Is all he could say as he looked at the body tied to the kitchen table.

"Guys please, me and my team first," Barrett gave the order. Freemond, Mercer and the captain stopped. After a couple of minutes all three walked outside, the captain pulled a hip flask and each took a quick swig.

Barrett came out a short time later, she had seen some crime scenes before but this was bad. "The mobile fingerprint says its Taylor Caine. Did you see the camera tripod and camera on the worktop?" All three cops shook their heads as a no. "The perp must have videoed whatever he did to her. Rough time of death…a couple of days ago, probably not long after the kidnapping. Why he shot her in the head then between the legs I don't know."

Mercer held back some sick, "Could the perp have known she was pregnant and be after the baby. Sick bastard."

"Maybe or maybe trying to hide possible rape D.N.A. I'll know when we get her back to the lab. I'm going first with the gun and the camera, the team will follow with the body later."

"I'll come with you, I should be near a medic with my possible concussion," Mercer said as he followed Barrett to a car. Before they got in two cars pulled up, jumping out of the first one was Frith. It took four uniforms to physically stop him heading for the house.

"I'm Carnello and Frith's lawyer. We were told this could be Taylor?"

The captain looked at the lawyer, ignored him and walked to the restrained Frith. "I am so sorry, Mr Frith, yes we believe it is Taylor. But you can't go in there."

Frith pulled two uniforms to the floor before Freemond put his gun to Frith's head. "Stay put big fella!"

Frith looked at Freemond, eyes glazed over with both drugs and tears. "Is my woman dead?"

"Let him go, Ray, put the gun down!" The captain placed himself between Freemond and the unrestrained Frith. "I am sorry, Mr Frith, but you have to let our forensics do their work."

Frith stared into the captain's eyes, and then took in the scene. "Why is Mercer covered in blood? Wait, is she holding a Desert Eagle?"

"Mercer nearly got our killer and yes we have the killer's gun. We will get him, Mr Frith, please." The captain pleaded.

The lawyer whispered something in Frith's ear then spoke, "Yes Captain, please do, but my client wishes to know what has gone on here and to see his girl."

"Yes of course, as soon as we can. Dobbs stay here with Mr Frith!"

Barrett and Mercer got in the car and drove off. Less than twenty minutes later Barrett opened her forensics room door. "I need the toilet, you can make the coffee, but don't wash, you may have evidence in your nails or on your clothes." Returning some fifteen minutes later Barrett found Mercer had made the coffee and was at the computer. "Anything?" She asked.

"No, just checking my mail. Sorry, should I log you back in?"

"Yes please, I'll get some fresh coffee. I have never reacted to a murder scene like this before."

Mercer looked at his partner, she was pale and he concluded she'd been sick in the toilet from the amount of time she had been in there. "Look, I'll take my jacket off carefully and with you being a medic I'll take a lie down on a slab. Do with me as you will." Barrett looked at her blood covered partner and did not wish to argue about not sleeping due to concussion.

The captain entered the lab, seeing his two detectives asleep on the slabs shouted, "Morning! You two sleeping together in my station!"

Mercer woke to his captain's voice. Sitting up, yawning he said, "Sorry Captain, I must have fallen asleep surprisingly." Mercer looked to his left, Barrett was just waking on the slab next to him.

"Morning you two, comfortable?" Freemond mocked.

"Get me a coffee and I'll talk." Barrett was off the slab and heading to her notes on her desk. "Whilst sleeping beauty was asleep I checked his clothes and fingernails. Not much there. The gun only has John's fingerprints on and the S.D. card from the camera is missing. No finger prints on that either."

"And the body?" The captain asked.

Barrett looked over to the third slab, Caine's body was on it. "Only a quick analysis, sorry, I was too tired. She is my next task."

Mercer looked at the third slab, "Did I really sleep next to a dead body? Now I do feel sick!" With that he went to the toilet. Mercer returned to see the captain had left but his friends were still in the room.

"Could you hold down some breakfast buddy?" Freemond asked.

"No," was Mercers simple reply.

Freemond continued, "Then let's leave Lisa to do her work, I need a full statement from you. To be honest anything you can recall may help catch this mother fucker." Mercer followed Freemond to the squad room. Within an hour he had formally debriefed, even giving as much of a description of his attacker as he could. Mercer wished to change the subject.

"And you buddy, the hospital?"

Freemond stopped and thought, "All was ok. Good results I'm as strong as an ox."

Mercer looked unsure at this answer. "Come on Ray, you can tell me. Whatever is going on here is nothing. You are all that matters."

"Thanks buddy. I'm ok really. Getting older but fit as I can be." Both cops sat and continued working for another hour. Freemond was concerned as Mercer complained of a headache. "Go home buddy. You could not have slept on that slab well."

"No, I'm fine. Besides is that not the lawyer from last night with the dickheads?"

Both cops watched as the trio went into the conference room, the captain called Mercer and Freemond in to the same room. Having entered they realised Barrett was already present with a tech guy. "Put it on Vids!" The captain ordered. Vids the tech guy took the S.D. card from the lawyer, placed it in a machine and pressed play. The screen showed the naked, alive, body of Taylor Caine tied to the kitchen table in half-light. Then a figure went between her legs, a short time later the gun was drawn. Some of the blood smudged the video camera and the final shot in between Caine's legs was heard but not seen.

The lawyer spoke, "Frith received this in the post this morning."

"Our perp is definitely after him. To video the killing is…" Barrett stopped. "Wait Vids, go back to when we see our perp." Vids rewound the footage to when part of the body could be seen between the victim's legs. "Freeze it! Look, our perp is a white male!"

All in the room looked at the screen, the captain spoke first. "You are right Barrett it does look that way. Can you analyse it further?"

"Yes, if that is all there is to watch right now I'll take it."

Jenks asked, "So if our perp is white why hide it. Why pretend to be black. Mercer you said he was black?"

"No, I said he looked black but it was a mask and gloves."

"How is Frith at the moment?" Head asked the lawyer.

The lawyer gulped, "He has been restrained, drugged even, and at a secure house. If he gets hold of this guy he will tear him to bits."

"So where does this lead us. The Pegasus connection, Olman dead as well?" The captain asked aloud.

"It would appear linked Captain," Ray stated the obvious. "I will get all I can on the gang through our records."

"Yes do that Ray. That will give Barrett time to assess the video and complete the autopsy on the body."

"I'll join him," Mercer said.

The captain ordered. "Jenks and Head, you two watch Frith. If he is the target then the perp has to go after him at some point. Go, all of you!"

A few hours passed, Mercer had downed too many aspirin for Freemond's liking. "You need to see a medic buddy!"

"I'm ok Ray, just all the paperwork, my eyes."

"Bullshit buddy that knock on your head was worse than we thought."

"Leave him Ray, I have some news!" Barrett had called as she headed to the captain's office. Mercer and Freemond followed.

The captain asked, "Barrett what you got?"

"First our victim had the Pegasus tattoo so she was involved with them in some way. No general evidence other than some pubic hair, we hopefully have our perp's D.N.A.!" Barrett had a smile.

"What do you mean, hopefully?" Mercer asked.

"Well assume she was seeing only Frith the male pubes I found were not his according to his D.N.A. on record."

"Then who the fuck are they from!" Freemond was a shouted reply rather than a question.

"I don't know as yet, it is going through the machine looking for matches. I'm checking all crooks, police and military records. Oh, I hope he is in there."

"How long, when?" The captain did not want to wait either.

"Patience, there are millions of records but if he is in our database it is only a matter of time." Barrett was confident. "Anything on the gang records? There can't have been many whites in Pegasus?"

Mercer replied, "No not yet. I think Caine was too young for the initial gang however, we know Frith loved the emblem and used it even after joining Carnello. It is his mark."

"Look you all go home, catch some sleep. I need you fresh for when that machine tells us something!" The captain looked at his team, "And that's an order!"

Chapter Eleven

Showdown

Frith circled the room; his head was full of menace. Whoever it was he was going to pull them apart bit by bit. As he circled, his gang mates kept aside, no one was going to argue with Frith in this mood. There was a beep of a cell message, "It's your cell, boss!" With that one of the gang members held Frith's cell up.

Frith took the cell phone and opened the message, his eyes got bigger and a grimace came to his mouth. He thought, and then shouted, "Play the video!"

"But boss…" The gang member did not finish as Frith pulled the controller from his fingers and pushed the man to the floor. Frith put the video of Taylor's death on and started to watch it. Then he froze it. Throwing the controller to the floor he ordered the gang member to give him his keys!" The gang member gave Frith the keys to his motorbike. Frith pushed aside two of his other goons, ignoring cries of, "Should we go with you!', and went to the garage. Mounting the Harley, Frith throttled it into life and took off, kicking open the part open garage doors. Seeing a police siren in his mirrors Frith throttled harder, losing the police car was easy on the bike.

The figure looked down at the high school entrance from the roof. Even though it was getting dark the figure could see the motorbike enter the school premises, alone. The figure watched as the rider got off the bike before entering the school doors.

Frith pushed open the school doors, gun drawn. He saw a body to his left. Frith stooped to check the body; the man was still breathing but was bound and gagged. The clothes suggested it was the caretaker. Frith knew the school and headed up the stairs to the third floor. Frith, seeing the classroom at the end to his right, did not care that it was the only lit room; he knew where he was headed.

Approaching the classroom Frith stopped, the door was ajar. Looking in he could just make out a figure sitting at the back of the classroom. Frith's blood boiled, he kicked open the classroom door, gun drawn he shouted, "Show yourself, you motherfucker!" The knock to his head made him fall.

Frith started to wake, his head hurt, he felt drowsy but he could see. He was still in the classroom. Frith got to his feet gingerly and looked to the rear of the classroom.

Two identical hooded figures were now sat at the last desks. Frith went for a weapon but he had none.

The figure spoke, "It did not take you long to realise." With that the figure pushed his right arm out striking the second figure, a dummy hit the floor. Frith looked at his prey, still sitting, still hooded, a gun on the desk in front of him. "I know it's you!"

The figure stood, removed the hood and Mercer spoke. "Our old teacher's house, we had many a time in there. We even played cards on that table."

"You sick mother fuck. You knew I would know the room, the house. And the text, *meet me at his workplace.* This is our schoolroom, that is your desk!"

Mercer picked up the gun, "No, this is Tanya's desk. You sat over there at the back, in the corner."

Frith looked to where his old desk was. "It's not changed much in what, Fifteen years or so?"

"Buying time with idle chit chat. I watched you come in you are alone. Oh by the way I did not just hit you but well I think it's called the date rape drug. Feeling drowsy?"

Frith did feel bad. "You bastard Mercer, what is all this about? Surely not some teenage fling I had with your girl?"

Mercer winced, held the gun up and pointed it at Frith as he walked towards him. "What else would it be about? You tried to take my girl!"

"What? No." Frith thought hard. "Look, you two weren't really tight when we met and yes I tried, but she chose you. We were kids."

"I have a long memory." Mercer sat on a desk just in front of Frith. "How did a shit like you get into my school and mix with good people like me and Tanya?"

"Good people like you?" Frith spat as he spoke.

"One train track between us, good my side, shit your side and a school in the middle. I guess even in those days someone pulled strings for you. Paid your bills."

"This is about us as school kids, no way!"

Mercer stood, pulled a knife from a holster and slashed Frith's leg; Frith fell to the floor shouting. "You fuck, let me wake up properly and give me a weapon. Fight like a man!"

Mercer struck again, pushing the knife into one arm, Frith tried to fight back but Mercer pushed his drugged body aside. Frith sat up on the floor, "Why the others? Why now?"

Mercer stood up, circling his prey. "Fernandez and Timo used to mock me. Remember when Tanya 'tried out your gang'? I had to pretend to join to keep an eye on things, but they just lied for you when you were with her. Now? Well it took time to get over my family's death, plus I learnt some IT skills, forensics even."

Tears came to Frith's eyes, "And Taylor, what did she do?"

Mercer struck out, cutting Frith's defending hands. "You didn't think Tanya would tell me. Did you?"

Frith was in agony but that comment hurt him more, "What do you know?"

"A few months before Tanya…passed, we had you on a wrap, you were going down. Tanya was the prosecutor's assistant, the first time you had met for years. You tried it on!" Mercer lashed out with another cut to Frith's body.

Frith was holding back the pain, but too much blood was leaving his body. "You fuck, that's not true!"

"I saw the texts, the flowers to her work and then you got off the wrap." Mercer kicked Frith in the groin before continuing, "You chased my girl again!"

"Kill me you deranged fuck!" Were the last words Frith spoke.

At the same time on the other side of the city Barrett had returned to work. "Ray, Ray you must meet me at John's!" Barrett shouted down the cell.

"I was just going to bed, Lisa. What's up, your machine told you something?" Freemond was unhappy.

"Just get to John's now!"

"Why John's…" Freemond stopped as the dial tone told him the call was over.

Freemond entered Mercer's building; Barrett was outside Mercer's apartment, gun drawn. "What the fuck are you up to Barrett?"

"Don't get silly, Ray. I think John is our perp, the killer!"

"What…no…why? I mean…"

"Trust me, he is. John are you in there?" Barrett shouted whilst knocking on the door. There was no reply, Barrett tried again. "John, it's me and Ray we just want to see how you are doing. Open the door please?"

A door opposite opened, an old lady looked out. "Hey, what is going on?" The lady asked. "Wait, you're that cop friend of John's?"

"Yes, Mrs Toan, I am."

"Why have you drawn your gun?"

"I think John is in trouble, do you have his key for emergencies?" Mrs Toan went and got the key and after handing it to Barrett went back and hid behind her door. Barrett and Freemond entered Mercer's apartment, both with guns drawn. Freemond was still confused but would support Barrett. Having checked the apartment was empty Freemond asked, "What are you on about Lisa?"

Barrett sat against the couch looking around the room then to her colleague. "I remembered when I saw Taylor's tattoo. John had one on his shoulder in the same place." As she spoke she looked at the wall where only a few days earlier she had seen the tattoo on Mercer's shoulder.

"No, Mercer's isn't a Pegasus tattoo, although I think it is a horse."

"It was a Pegasus but changed and generally made bigger. Tanya had the same tattoo remember?"

Freemond thought, "Maybe, yes it could have been a changed Pegasus. You mean John and Tanya were in Olman's gang?"

Barrett thought, "I'm not sure but the link made me think, so I checked my records. John's file had been changed on my computer twice. Once to remove his

D.N.A. and fingerprint records then the second to put his fingerprint records back on."

Freemond fell into a chair, "No. No. Not John. Oh my god, why?"

"I don't have the whole story but John and Frith knew each other before and Tanya…" Before Barrett finished her sentence Freemond's cell rang.

"Hello, what? No. Yes Captain." Freemond ended the call. "That was the captain he is on his way to the hospital. Merce has taken Moore hostage." Both cops went in one car taking the trip to the hospital.

Entering the ward that Moore was on Barrett and Freemond met the captain and the DA, Maygan. "I don't know what Mercer is up to but he has a gun to Moore's head and demanded to see me and the D.A.!"

"Captain, I think John is our killer!"

The captain froze as Barrett delivered these words. "No, surely not?" He said in disbelief.

Freemond backed up his colleague, "From what Lisa has said in the car on the way over here and the evidence she has. It is Merce."

"Captain. Mercer wants to speak to you and the D.A. something about a deal?" A uniform said.

The captain looked at D.A. Maygan, "Are you ok with this?"

Maygan replied, "Hell I don't know what is going on here but he would not shoot you and me?"

The captain and D.A. walked to the outside of Moore's private room. The door was shut but the window to the main ward had been smashed by an earlier shot from Mercer. The captain and the D.A. stood in the window. Looking in the captain could see Mercer was standing in a corner with a gun to Moore's head, whom he was holding tightly in front of him. "John, what is going on?"

Mercer responded, "Sorry Captain, but there is something you and the D.A. need to know."

"Then tell us and maybe we can do a deal. But only if you don't harm Detective Moore!" Maygan stated.

"Tell them Moore. Tell them the truth!" Mercer pushed the gun barrel into Moore's ear as he spoke.

"Tell them what Merce? What?" Moore squealed.

"The truth about Tanya and Maddie!" Mercer again pushed the gun into Moore's ear but harder.

"Ouch! Ok, Ok!" Moore continued, "The car crash it was a set up, the drunk bum was just a clever cover."

Mercer tightened his grip around Moore's throat, "And the rest, tell them who!"

"It was Frith, he organised it all, he had Tanya and Maddie killed."

"And!" Mercer pushed.

"And I was paid to cover it up. I am so sorry, Captain," With this Moore broke into tears.

Freemond and Barrett joined the captain and the D.A. at the window. Barrett spoke, "Oh John, I am so sorry. Please let Moore go and we can talk about this?"

The D.A. thought, and then supported Barrett, "Detective Mercer, I have no idea of what has been going on or your involvement but let Detective Moore go. I will do you a deal. I promise!"

Mercer smiled, Freemond shouted, "John, please, no. You have killed shit so far don't add a police officer to the…" Freemond's words were interrupted by the sound of the gun. As Moore was dropped, Mercer shot at the D.A.

Freemond, Barrett and the captain acted instinctively, pulling their guns and shooting Mercer.

Chapter Twelve

The Funeral

The hearse pulled up inside the cemetery. The ceremony had taken place and the occupants, Barrett, Freemond and his wife, Gloria, got out for the burial. Captain Ward opened Barrett's door.

"Thank you Captain." Barrett said as he took her hand.

"I'm sorry we could not make the church. Mercer, well you know he is not being buried with police honours. Ray, Mrs Freemond." The captain also welcomed his colleague and wife. Following the coffin the group walked towards the open grave. As they got in sight of the grave Barrett saw some fifteen colleagues, not in uniform, but present at the graveside nevertheless. "It may not be official but many of the team wanted to recognise Mercer and pay their respects. He was a good cop before this recent tragedy." The captain advised.

The ceremony was brief, no full honours although Freemond placed Mercer's badge on the coffin. Each of the police colleagues said something or just shook Barrett and Freemond's hands before they left. Murphy spoke to Barrett, "I am still in shock, John was a lovely guy but...look the wake is at my place we will catch you there." Giving Barrett an embrace he then left.

A stranger, who had been at the edge of the ceremony, walked up to Barrett and said, "Hi, I am Colonel Matthews. I was in the marines with Jack Mercer, John's father. Once we heard I had to at least acknowledge another fallen hero. I heard John had his father's attention to detail and lack of fear."

Barrett smiled at the colonel, "Thank you. Yes he did. Unfortunately I did not know John's father that well but I did meet him a few times. You were at his funeral, and Tanya's now I recall."

"Yes. Sad, sad times. I thought Tanya's parents would be here?

Barett replied, "No they are ill and could not make the journey, but did send a message and flowers."

"I've not seen Steph in some time, is she still in the home?"

"Yes. She has been told but does not wish to acknowledge John's death."

"Look I am happy to see her tomorrow. Maybe you could go with my wife and I? Her and Steph got on well together."

"Yes. Any help would be appreciated." Barrett gave the colonel a quick hug., taking a contact card from him. As the colonel was walking away Barrett shouted, "Did John's father have a Dessert Eagle?"

The colonel stopped, thought and turned to address Barrett, "Yes why?"

"Nothing, nothing really but thank you again."

Captain Ward shook Freemond's hand and embraced Barrett, whispering in her ear, "I can't forget the last few weeks but John was a good cop. He was a good husband and a good father. Only remember the best of him as I will try to." The captain then took Mrs Freemond's arm, "Mrs Freemond, may I?"

"Yes of course," Gloria Freemond replied. "Lisa, honey, you have a moment alone with Ray. We will see you at Murphy's." With that the captain and Mrs Freemond left.

Barrett and Freemond took a few steps back. Barrett looked at the three graves in front of them. There was the unfilled Mercer grave, Tanya's and the smaller child-sized one between them. Barrett started to sob. Freemond gave her a hug, "Let's sit down for a minute on that bench."

Freemond led Barratt to the bench and they both sat. Freemond continued, "Hell I can't agree with John's actions but when you look at this. I would want revenge as well."

"He must have planned this for some time, even getting the D.A. to the hospital. Another money taking shit! He as the prosecutor at the time was paid off by Frith to throw the crash case. And the made up fight at Olman's." Barrett thought, having had sleepless nights over the last few days since Mercer was taken. "He could have gotten away with it. He just had to be more careful. Is it wrong to think that, Ray?"

Freemond thought before answering, "Look Lisa, it is clear now the Olman link was not planned for, maybe the only off the cuff action he took. Killing the gang hoodlums is one thing…but to get Caine, Moore and the D.A. is another. Besides I would think that once the job was done, dying to be with Tanya and Maddie was his goal."

"He made us kill him?"

Freemond started to cry, "Yes, maybe planned, maybe not, but he was out of his mind by then."

Barrett looked up at the sky, her head trying to take in all the previous events. "Why did John not speak to us Ray? We could have helped?"

"Oh Lisa. I'm sure he knew we would help but I'd guess he had no faith in the system. A system that let him down in his moment of need."

"He must have been so cut up inside, so tormented, to do this."

"It's hard I know, but forget the last few weeks as the captain said. John was a good man. He is up there now where he wanted to be with Tanya and little Maddie." Freemond looked at Barrett and added, "Hey, he loved us as well."

Barrett wiped her eyes, gave her friend a smile and a quick peck on the cheek and said, "Thanks."

The End

Ken Kirkberry books:

Enlightenment young adult/coming of age Sci fi trilogy:

Enlightenment: This Earth
Enlightenment: Another Earth
Enlightenment: Colliding Earths

Find out more:

https://www.amazon.co.uk/Ken-Kirkberry/e/B0722YXS97/ref=sr_ntt_srch_lnk_1?qid=1523824003&sr=8-1

https://www.facebook.com/ken.kirkberry.9

Printed in Great Britain
by Amazon

32685120R00093